BONDED BY DARKNESS

The Literary Yogi

INKSTATE

ISBN 978-93-5559-004-6
Copyright © Venugopal Balasubramanian, 2021

First published in India 2021 by Leadstart Inkstate
A brand of One Point Six Technologies Pvt. Ltd.

123, Building J2, Shram Seva Premises,
Wadala Truck Terminal,
Mumbai 400022, Maharashtra, INDIA
Phone: +91 96999 33000
Email: info@leadstartcorp.com
www.leadstartcorp.com

Disclaimer: This is a work of fiction. All the names, characters, businesses,
places, events and incidents in this book are either the product of the author's
imagination or used in a fictitious manner. Any resemblance to actual persons,
living or dead, or actual events is purely coincidental.

Editor: Roona Ballachanda
Cover: R. Maharaja
Layouts: Ashwini Rane

For my son, Leonardo, who inspires me and makes me want to be a better person everyday.

P.S: Mom, please skip over the sex scenes.

CONTENTS

ACKNOWLEDGEMENTS

I want to start by thanking my wife, Carisa, and my son, Leonardo, for being the most incredible family I could have asked for. I would like to thank my mom and sister for motivating me to move forward. I would like to thank my dad, who is not with me anymore, for nurturing my creativity. Last but not the least, I would like to thank the Leadstart family for being a partner every step of the way in getting this novel in front of you.

ABOUT THE AUTHOR

Father to an incredible little man, husband to wonder woman, storyteller, and someone who treats others like he wants to be treated. The author will be writing under the pen name, The Literary Yogi. Yogi was a name the author's parents chose to give him at birth because he looked like he had achieved inner peace. He is forty and is struggling with accepting the appearance of grey hairs on his head. He grew up in India and currently lives in Atlanta, in the United States. Even though this is his first time writing a novel, he has been writing throughout his life either through helping friends write assignments, writing scripts for interschool and intercollegiate plays, or writing numerous papers over the course of his life. When he is not writing, his life revolves around his family and his job. He is an avid soccer player, a global traveler, and the chef of the house.

CHAPTER ONE

DEATH IS CERTAIN; THE TIME IS UNCERTAIN

February 2018, Mumbai, India

The diverse inhabitants of Mumbai fondly called it the city of dreams and the city that never slept. A hodge-podge of culture, fashion, food, and people, Mumbai was a global metropolis. Home to iconic financial institutions like the Reserve Bank of India and the Bombay Stock Exchange, it served as the financial powerhouse of India. The pizzazz of Bollywood, the largest sector of the Indian film industry, drew people from all over the country, people who wanted to be immersed in the glamor of the silver screen.

An old white van with tinted windows cruised down an empty road. Beethoven's "Fur Elise" echoed from its speakers. The van turned a corner and pulled over on the side of the road at Nariman Point, a business district in downtown Mumbai. Located at the southern tip of the Mumbai peninsula and on one end of Mumbai's marine drive, Nariman Point was one of the most expensive locations for commercial real estate in the world.

The first passenger in the van was Leonardo Varma. He sat in the driver's seat and stared at a skyscraper across the street. Leo was dressed in a three-piece pinstriped suit and wore a salt-and-pepper wig. He also wore a matching moustache and beard and green contact lenses, along with a pair of wire-rimmed glasses. This morning he would play the role of Oberoi, a rich industrialist from

London who wanted to invest in real estate in Mumbai.

The second passenger was Isabella Basu. She sat in the passenger seat of the van and was dressed in a three-piece black suit and a tweed golf cap. She wore a black wig underneath her cap and had on a moustache and beard that matched her hair color. She was disguised as O'Malley, Oberoi's Irish bodyguard. Her Irish accent wasn't convincing at all, which wasn't a problem, because she didn't have to talk as O'Malley.

The third person who was seated behind the driver's seat was Sebastian George. He held a large mug of coffee and looked nervous. Sebastian wore dark blue overalls with the logo of the local internet provider embossed on it. He also wore a beige hat with the Porsche logo etched into it. He was a mechanical whiz, and his expertise was going to be critical to the success of the day's operation.

The fourth passenger was Walt. He wore dark blue overalls and held a chocolate-frosted donut in one hand and a cup of coffee in the other. He bit off a large chunk of the donut and washed it down with a swig of coffee. He appeared the least nervous of the group.

The neon sign in front of the skyscraper across the street flashed bright green. The parking lot in the skyscraper was now open to customers. Leo drove the van through the entrance to the parking garage. The bottom five floors of the skyscraper consisted of parking garages. Anyone willing to pay the exorbitant fees could use them. The sixth floor housed the food court, which contained an eclectic mix of global fast food chains and local restaurants. The rest of the floors were filled with corporate offices. The people who worked in those offices were considered the best in their professions.

Leo drove the van onto the fifth floor and pulled into a parking spot that offered an exquisite view of the Arabian Sea. The passengers of the van opened their doors and stepped out of the van. The four passengers who were reborn in the fires of adversity would be bonded forever after the day's incidents transpired. They stood side by side and stared into the ocean. It was early in the morning, and the hustle and bustle of life hadn't started in full swing yet.

By the water stood the Royal Global Bank building in all its grandeur. The clientele of the bank were men and women who were the elite of society. Clients included people who had inherited fortunes, people who had created successful businesses from scratch, top athletes, politicians, and people who made their money by exploitation, murder, and any other crime one could imagine. The bank prided itself for its affluence and showed it off by erecting a structure like none other. The façade of the building was sixty feet tall and eighty feet wide and made of marble. Twenty-foot high bronze double doors allowed entry and exit.

Two guards wearing black uniforms and armed with holstered Magnum Research Desert Eagle .50 caliber handguns stood guard on either side of the majestic double doors. Statues of majestic lions sat on either side of the double doors. The statues signified power and majesty, the defining principles of the bank. A state-of-the-art helicopter with the logo of the bank painted on its side sat atop the third-floor roof of the bank.

Leo grabbed a rolled-up sheet of paper from the back of the van. "Today we embark on a journey that will transform our lives one way or another. Are you ready to rob the only bank you will ever rob?" Leo gazed at his partners in crime. A lump formed in his throat.

His question was met with silence. Isa broke the silence. "Never in my wildest dreams did I ever imagine doing something like this. That said, I wouldn't consider doing this if the three of you weren't by my side." Isa took Leo's hand in hers as their gazes met. "I'm ready," said Isa.

Sebastian sighed.

Leo unrolled the sheet of paper he was holding and laid it on the hood of the van. "Let's go over the plan one last time. Cell phone jammer, check?" Leo looked at Sebastian.

Sebastian brushed his clammy hands against his overalls leaving moist spots on both thighs. "Check. Walt and I tested it this morning, and it worked great. We are good to go."

Leo looked at Sebastian and then Walt. "Fiber-optic cables check?"

Walt took a swig of coffee. "Sebastian and I went by our spot earlier this morning and ensured that we still have access to the fiber optic cables carrying internet to the bank. Let's just say once we are done with the cables, people in the bank won't be sending any emails," said Walt with a sheepish grin.

Leo placed his hand on Walt's shoulder. "Or sounding the intruder alarm?"

"Or that." Walt laughed as he chomped on another donut.

Sebastian blew into his sweaty palms. "Why are you not nervous, Walt?"

"Sugar, my brother," said Walt, holding up the rest of the donut. "I am also focusing on the present, since I have no control over what happens in the future. This keeps me from freaking out." Walt took a large bite.

Isa jabbed Walt in the arm. "Sound advice. What have you done with Walt?"

Isa's light-hearted comment made everyone smile. Walt gave Isa a stern look before taking a bow.

"What about your gas contraption?" Isa asked as she gently laid a black box on the hood of the van.

The box was eight inches long, six inches wide, and three inches deep. Walt sighed. "I have tested it as best as I could. If the light on the remote turns green, the gas was released." Walt handed Isa the remote. Sebastian and Walt had engineered the device to release enough gas to knock out people within a ten-foot radius.

"Got it. Green is great, red is dead." Isa gently took the device off the hood and placed it inside the van.

"Really hope we don't need to use it," said Leo. He cracked his knuckles and took a deep breath.

If everything went according to plan, Isa and Leo would be in and out of the bank in less than an hour. On the sides of the van, Sebastian and Walt put stickers with logos of the local internet and cellular provider. Leo and Isa got in the back of the van. Sebastian got in the driver's seat, and Walt jumped into the passenger seat. The bank would open shortly, time for the plan to be in motion.

The sun kissed the sparkling ocean on its journey beyond the horizon. "This could be the last time we get to enjoy this picturesque view," said Isa with concern in her voice. "If we are caught, we will be arrested." She sighed.

Leo adjusted his tie. "With the amount of heat the security guards are packing, if our operation goes south, this will be the last time we get to see any view," He immediately regretted saying it out aloud.

Walt turned to face Leo and shook his head. "Way to inspire confidence."

Leo tried to do damage control. "Isa and I will be in and out as planned, and we will toast to our victory. Let's go forth and change our lives." Leo's voice was steady.

"Can you drop us at our rendezvous point, mate?" Leo asked in his makeshift cockney accent. "How is my accent? Think I will pass for a Brit?"

Walt turned to face Leo. "You sound like an Englishman who spent a lot of time in Australia."

Isa and Sebastian burst out laughing.

Leo shook his head. It was a welcome comment and took away some of the anxiety, even if for a few brief moments.

Sebastian drove the van out of the building and stopped.

Leo extended out his palm. "Let's kick the tires and light the fires." The others put their palms on top.

Isa and Leo got out of the van and waited on the side of the road. Sebastian drove the van a short distance ahead and pulled over on the side of the road. Isa rolled a large briefcase, and Leo held the gas contraption that Walt and Sebastian had built. There was a lot of activity on the street. People wearing suits and yelling into their cell phones were everywhere. Isa and Leo fit right into the sea of corporate professionals. It was a short car ride to the bank from where Leo and Isa stood. An elegant white Rolls Royce Phantom pulled up in front of the building. Leo walked toward the car and pulled out a laminated red card from his jacket pocket. He waved it at the driver, who came out of the car immediately.

The driver got out of the car and saluted Leo and Isa. "Good morning, sir. Thank you for being a customer of our luxury rental service." He took the laminated card from Leo and scanned it on a device on the dashboard. "I will be at your service for the next four hours, sir." The driver returned the card to Leo. Leo thanked the driver. The driver opened the trunk for Isa and placed the large briefcase inside. He shut the trunk and circled around the car to open the rear door. The luxury rental company was perfect for the operation because it dealt in cash and didn't need to have a credit card on file. Leo provided it a copy of his fake passport and the cash it had requested in return for the luxury car and driver. The fees charged by the rental company were steep, but the stylish car gave the impression of affluence.

The driver turned back to look at Leo. "Where is our first stop, sir?"

"Take us to the Royal Global Bank," said Leo in his cockneyish accent.

"Your wish is my command, sir. There are beverages in the cooler under the seat, sir," said the driver, eager to please.

The Rolls Royce drove toward the bank. Sebastian followed it in the van and kept a safe distance. The car turned into the gate of the bank and pulled up at the front entrance. The driver got out and opened the doors for Leo and Isa. He then opened the trunk and retrieved the briefcase. He handed it to Isa.

Sebastian parked the van outside the bank. He made sure it wasn't visible to the security guards in front of the bank doors.

One of the security guards walked up to the Rolls Royce. "Please pull the car around the back and wait in the parking lot," the security guard said to the driver.

The driver got in the car.

If everything went as planned, the Rolls Royce would take Isa and Leo out of the bank in a short while.

The second security guard came down the steps. "Can I see some identification, sir?"

Leo reached into his jacket and handed his fake British passport to the guard who looked at the photo page and then at Leo. The guard then took the fake Irish passport from Isa and quickly examined it. "Welcome, Mr. Oberoi and Mr. O'Malley. Do you have any weapons?" The guard handed back their passports.

Leo pointed at Isa. "I don't, but my bodyguard does."

The security guard addressed Isa. "You will need to drop off your weapons at the security desk before you enter the bank, sir. You will get them back when you leave." The guard opened the thick double doors. "Welcome to Royal Global Bank."

Isa nodded.

The guard closed the door once Leo and Isa were through, Leo set his watch to countdown twenty minutes. Leo and Isa walked down the long hallway that led to the reception desk.

Outside, Sebastian had positioned himself where he had visibility of the majestic bronze double doors through the bank gate. Once Leo and Isa were through the doors and the doors were fully shut, he set his watch to countdown twenty minutes. He then walked to the van.

The man who stood behind the reception desk wore a black suit and dark rimmed glasses. "Welcome to the Royal Global Bank, Mr. Oberoi and Mr. O'Malley."

Leo turned to look at the bronze double doors. "How thick are those doors?"

"Eight inches thick and sound-proof, sir." The man behind the reception looked at the doors and beamed. "There could be an explosion outside and we wouldn't even know it happened."

"Impressive." Leo glanced at the two burly men on either side of the reception area. Both giant security guards wore black suits and had AR-15 rifles slinging from their shoulders and 9mm handguns holstered on either side at their hips. The guards had cold eyes, grim expressions, and an eerie calmness about them. These men wouldn't hesitate to use their firearms if anything went wrong.

Leo's thoughts were interrupted by the man behind the reception desk. "May I see some identification, sir?" The man extended his right hand.

Leo handed him his fake passport, as did Isa.

The man looked at the photo pages and seemed satisfied. "What is the purpose of your visit?" He handed Leo and Isa back their passports.

"I live in London and plan to invest in real estate in Mumbai. I need a reliable financial institution to handle my money. Your bank came highly recommended for its thoroughness and more importantly, its discretion. I will be opening an account I can manage from anywhere in the world. I will be depositing cash and diamonds." Leo gestured to the large leather briefcase Isa rolled.

"You have made the right choice, sir," said the man behind the reception. "May I please see the items you want to deposit?" He glanced at the briefcase.

Leo handed the man a pouch of fake diamonds, which he opened and checked quickly. "Someone upstairs will check how much the diamonds are worth." The man handed the diamonds back to Leo. "May I see the cash please, sir?" Isa opened the box and showed it to the man. The man was satisfied with what he saw. "Thank you, sir. The manager will check everything thoroughly upstairs. Are either of you carrying any weapons?"

"I am not a weapons guy, but my man O'Malley over here always packs heat." The man behind the reception turned to Isa. "He is a gun enthusiast and collector" said Leo.

"Please hand me your weapons, Mr. O'Malley. You can put them in this box, and you will receive them at the exit desk when you leave." The man placed a large wooden box lined with blue velvet on the desk.

Isa took out two impeccable Glock 17 replicas from holsters inside her suit lapels and placed them carefully in the box. One of the giant security guards looked at the guns and gave Isa a nod. Isa acknowledged the big man. The guard then went back to staring at the double doors.

Leo chuckled. "I couldn't tell if they were statues or were alive."

"They are men of few words, Mr. Oberoi, but they are the best. Lastly, I will need your cell phones to be placed in the box." The man grabbed the box with both hands and held it up.

Leo reached into his blazer to retrieve his phone. "Wow, no cell phones?"

The man behind the reception shrugged. "Only employees are allowed cell phones, sir. We don't permit any communication devices in the bank, including cell phones, smart watches, and tablets among other things."

Isa and Leo placed their cell phones inside the box next to the guns. "Well in that case, I'll leave my tablet in the care of you gentlemen," said Leo. He gently placed the black box with chemicals inside the wooden box.

The man behind the reception eyed the object Leo placed in the box. "That is a large device, Mr. Oberoi."

"The device itself is small, but the cover is huge. I got the most durable cover which makes the device fire and water proof. An elephant could step on it, and the device inside wouldn't get a scratch. It also comes in handy to knock someone out." Leo chucked. He hoped there wouldn't be further discussion about the device.

The man put a label with the name Mr. Oberoi in the box. He put the box on a conveyer belt and pushed a button. The belt started to move. "Where does the belt go?" Leo acted impressed.

"There is an exit desk with the same system as here." The man gestured to the wall behind him with his thumb. "My peer who works at the exit desk will retrieve it from the belt and place it on his desk. Before you leave, you will need to show him identification, and you will get your items back."

The man pushed a button and a wrought iron door popped open. He pulled the door fully open and pushed another button on the wall. A metal door slid open revealing an elevator. "The elevator will take you up to the bank lobby." The man showed Leo and Isa into the elevator. "Thank you for your business, sir." He bid Leo and Isa farewell.

Leo checked his watch after the elevator door closed. "Twelve minutes down, eight to go, Isa." The elevator came to a halt after a moment.

A stocky man waited for Leo and Isa outside the elevator. "Good morning, Mr. Oberoi, I am Sharma, the manager of the bank." Sharma extended both hands and shook Leo's hand. "Thank you for choosing us as your partner."

He then shook Isa's hand with both his hands.

"This is our receptionist, Ruby." Sharma introduced the young woman with glasses seated behind a large carved oak desk.

"Namaste." Ruby joined her palms together and leaned her head forward slightly. "Welcome to the Royal Global Bank," she said with a large smile.

Leo and Isa joined their palms and leaned forward. Ruby appeared delighted with their gesture.

The manager strutted past the reception desk. "I would like to give you a quick tour before we get down to business. Please allow me to show you our lobby. We are immensely proud of our lobby, the likes of which doesn't exist anywhere else in the country." He gestured for Leo and Isa to follow him. "A Spanish architect designed the lobby to pay homage to her idol, the high renaissance artist, Michelangelo. The art on the walls and the ceiling mimics the Sistine Chapel in the Vatican." Sharma swelled with pride. "The mesmerizing building is inspired by the Duomo di Milano, the Milan Cathedral, which was designed by an Italian architect renowned for using gothic architecture. The gothic style that flourished in Europe during the medieval period was aesthetically baroque and abstractly transcendent and became one of the most idiosyncratic architectural movements." Sharma gloated at his flawless delivery.

"Wow. How long did it take you to learn all that?" Leo chuckled. "This is stunning." Leo stared at the ceiling in awe. Isa had been here before, but Leo hadn't. It was difficult not to be wonderstruck by such architectural beauty, and Leo lost track of time. Isa nudged Leo, and he looked at his watch. It had been seventeen minutes since they entered the double doors. They were right on schedule, and it was time to go into Sharma's office.

"Incredible, Mr. Sharma. You have truly bedazzled me with the splendor of this lobby. I feel transported to Rome, to the Vatican." Leo soaked in the vivid colors and ornate frescoes. "We are ready to talk business, Mr. Sharma."

"Please follow me to my office." Sharma pointed to a carved oak door in the corner of the lobby. He walked toward the door and Leo and Isa followed. Sharma held the oak door open and Isa and Leo entered his office. "Please have a seat." Sharma gestured to two plush leather chairs in front of his large oak desk.

Leo looked at his watch, which showed the countdown at eighteen minutes. The moment of truth was almost there. Sharma sat on his plush leather chair. Leo walked to the window that overlooked the ocean. "Breathtaking view, Mr. Sharma." Leo looked out into the ocean. "Something I couldn't find in London even if I paid through my nose."

"I would switch places with you in a heartbeat, Mr. Oberoi." Sharma chuckled. He stood up and walked to the window. Isa grabbed the walkie-talkie from Sharma's desk. The twenty-minute countdown was done, as Leo's watch beeped thrice.

Downstairs in the white van, Sebastian gave Walt the signal. Walt activated the powerful cell phone signal jammer. He looked at his phone and gave Sebastian the thumbs up. He had disrupted phone communications for everyone within a two-block radius. Walt knew the jammer worked when he saw people on the street stare at their phones, confused and frustrated.

Sebastian stood at the spot where he would access the fiber optic cables carrying internet to the bank. The powerful battery-operated saw buzzed when he powered it on. Sebastian had already cut a hole in the concrete, which gave him access to the cables that ran three feet underground. He removed the square piece of concrete he had placed on top of the hole and saw the cables. He knelt on the ground and maneuvered the saw. It sliced through the cables with ease, rendering the bank without internet.

"Listen to me carefully, Mr. Sharma," said Leo in his regular accent. "This is a heist, and we are going to walk out of here with money and diamonds."

Sharma was distraught. With a look of disbelief, he lunged to his desk. "Why is the alarm system not working?" Sharma was hysterical as he pushed the button underneath his desk over and over. "What is happening? Why are the alarms not working?" He whimpered as he punched keys on his cell phone frantically. "Where is my walkie-talkie?" He scrambled as he looked for his walkie-talkie.

"Calm down Sharma," said Leo. "My team has taken out your internet and jammed everyone's cell phones in a two-block radius. Both your internet and cell phone alarm systems are disabled. The only way for you to communicate with security downstairs is using your walkie-talkie."

Isa held up the walkie-talkie. "Your bank is disconnected from the world temporarily. Please have a seat. No one needs to get hurt."

Leo sat down in the plush leather chair.

Sharma collapsed into his chair and turned pale. "You don't know how dangerous the people who own the bank and our clients are." Sharma gained his composure. "They will find and destroy you and everyone that matters to you."

Isa pulled open a hidden compartment in the rolling case and took out a device. It consisted of a timer attached to a glass canister. The canister was filled with a bright blue liquid. She hit a switch on the device and placed it on the table. The timer on the device counted down.

"We appreciate your concern for us," said Leo. He leaned forward and put his elbows on Sharma's desk. "If you don't cooperate, O'Malley will release the nerve gas in the canister. We are carrying enough gas to kill everyone in the bank. Once the nerve gas is inhaled, it kills in a matter of minutes, extremely painful minutes. It triggers violent convulsions and the body shuts down. Death is slow and painful by asphyxiation. Think about your kids and your family and the families of all the people who work at the bank." Leo's eyes bored into Sharma. "My associate and I have gas masks that will protect us." Isa took gas masks out of the rolling briefcase.

Sharma hyperventilated.

"We could release the gas and walk out of here without being impacted. You will do exactly as we say, and no one will get hurt," said Leo.

"What do you want me to do?" Sharma asked in a feeble voice.

"Call your secretary on the walkie-talkie and tell her there is an internet and cell phone outage. Your provider for both these services emailed you earlier this morning, but you forgot about it. Tell her to let security know everything is okay. Is that clear?" Leo asked.

Sharma extended his shaky hand. Isa handed Sharma the walkie-talkie. Sharma called his secretary and did as he was told.

Leo got up from the chair. "Good. Now open the vault and give us what we need. We will be on our way after that." Leo and Isa put on the gas masks.

"You won't get away with this." Sharma mumbled as he walked to the vault.

"Let's make sure everyone here doesn't die first," said Leo through the gas mask.

Sharma reached the vault and punched in the code. The vault door opened. It was lined with hundreds of lockers. Leo and Isa followed Sharma into the vault. Isa emptied the fake British pounds and diamonds from the briefcase onto the vault floor. She loaded the briefcase with cash and some diamonds.

Isa closed the briefcase and rolled it out of the vault. "If we don't leave right away, we will miss our rendezvous at the pier." Isa looked at her watch.

Leo threw his arms up but said nothing to Isa. He turned to Sharma. "Pleased doing business with you." Leo locked Sharma inside the vault. Leo and Isa took off their masks and put them inside the briefcase. Isa took the device from Sharma's desk and threw it into the briefcase. The alleged nerve gas in the canister was harmless blue dye. Isa took Sharma's walkie-talkie and put it in his trashcan under a mound of paper.

"By the look on his face, I think he bought your comment about us going to the pier," said Leo as he opened Sharma's office door.

Sharma's assistant bid them goodbye.

"How do we get to the exit elevator?" Leo asked. Sharma's assistant showed Leo where the elevator was. Leo thanked her and walked to the elevator.

Sharma's assistant walked into Sharma's office.

"We have to use Walt's gas contraption." Leo had a hint of panic in his voice. "We don't have much time before Sharma gets to the security guards." The elevator doors closed. "We need to knock out the guards. I was hoping we wouldn't need to."

Isa took the remote from her jacket and pushed the only button on it. The light on the remote went green. "Green is great," said Isa. Leo and Isa put on their gas masks and hoped for the best.

Leo's heart beat rapidly. "If the device didn't work, it could be the end." The elevator door opened to a cloud of gas. "Walt's crazy contraption worked." Leo and Isa waited for a short while to ensure the gas did what it was engineered to do. "Let's go." Leo stepped out of the elevator first. Leo and Isa walked down the passage to the double doors and stopped halfway to remove their masks.

Leo felt a sharp pain in his right arm and gasped as he hit the ground. One of the large security guards had fired a few shots from his 9 mm gun before he was knocked out. One of the shots hit Leo in his right arm.

Isa trembled. "Are you ok?" She helped Leo up.

Leo took off his jacket. "The pain is awful, but we are almost there. Can you tape around the wound? I don't want to bleed all over the car." Blood had soaked into his shirt.

Isa taped the wound with duct tape. "Glad I brought the tape in case we needed to detain someone. We'll get you medical attention as soon as we are in the clear." Isa looked pained.

Leo put on his jacket and resumed a poker face. "Let's get this over with. I am fine" He opened the heavy brass door. He waved to the driver, and the majestic white Rolls Royce pulled up to the door. The driver jumped out and opened the door.

Leo waved to the security guards. "Thank you." He got into the luxurious car. It pulled out of the bank gate and headed to the pier. Leo turned around and saw Sebastian and Walt follow in the van.

Sharma's secretary searched for Sharma. She thought he was using the restroom and decided to come back later. She suddenly heard thumps coming from the vault. When she listened carefully, she distinctly heard Sharma's voice from inside the vault. She ran out of Sharma's office and got the assistant manager, who was the only other person in the building who could open the vault. The assistant manager opened the vault and Sharma ran out.

"We've been robbed, I need my walkie-talkie," screamed Sharma as he ran to his desk. He frantically looked for his walkie-talkie but couldn't find it. "Where is your walkie-talkie?" Sharma asked the assistant manager.

The assistant manager stuttered. "In my office, sir."

Sharma ran to the assistant manager's office and grabbed his walkie-talkie. He called the exit reception desk, but no one answered. He then called the guards outside the exit double doors. "Stop the two men in suits," he yelled. "We've been robbed."

"Too late, sir," said one of the guards. "Their white Rolls Royce drove out of the gate a short while ago."

Sharma called the reception desk and asked the two large security guards to meet him at the rooftop. He ran to the rooftop, where he was met by the security guards. Sharma got into the eight-seater Augusta Westland AW119 helicopter that belonged to the bank. "The thieves are headed to the pier," said Sharma. "We might still be able to get them." The helicopter roared to life as the pilot started it. "They are in a white Rolls Royce." Sharma screamed to be heard over the loud noise caused by the blades. Sharma spotted the white Rolls Royce at the pier. As the helicopter circled the pier, a Yamaha speedboat glided into the ocean with a roar.

"Follow the boat," screamed Sharma. "I can see the thieves. Oberoi, the one wearing the pinstriped suit, is driving the boat. His bodyguard with the black suit is sitting beside him." He moved to the edge of his seat. "Got the bastards. No one can rob the Royal Global Bank and get away with it," he screamed with a newfound relief in his voice.

The helicopter caught up with the boat. Sharma asked the security guards to fire warning shots into the water. The boat sped up with a loud roar and lost control, crashing into a huge rock formation. There was a loud explosion as debris flew everywhere and landed in the ocean.

Sharma reeled from the explosion with a look of disbelief on his face. There was nothing left of the boat or its passengers. Sharma let out a loud scream of agony. "It's over. Let's head back to the pier." Sharma sank into his seat and buried his face in his palms.

Sharma's secretary called the police and informed them about the robbery.

The helicopter landed in an open area in the pier and Sharma got out. Police sirens blared all over the pier.

CHAPTER TWO

FINDING PURPOSE

Mumbai, August 2016

Bandra West, a stylish suburb of Mumbai, is a confluence of ancient and modern worlds. Its preserved seventeenth-century architecture contrasted starkly with its chic cafes and upscale global restaurants and bars.

Leo moved to Mumbai after he learned the devastating truth about his mother's death. He had received a letter eight months earlier on his twenty-first birthday that filled him with rage and abhorrence toward his father. Leo didn't confront his father before he left because he was afraid of what he might do to him. He needed to escape his old life and decided that Mumbai was going to be his new home. He ended up in Mumbai because it was the cosmopolitan capital and because of its proximity to the ocean. His mother wasn't by his side, but she had left him a good-sized inheritance that gave him financial flexibility.

Situated in the charming neighborhood of Bandra West was Transform, a state-of-the-art fitness club. Leo worked as a mixed martial arts instructor and a personal trainer in Transform. He was one of the most popular personal trainers and had an eclectic group of clients.

Leo had been introduced to a mixed martial arts fight club by one of his clients. After a lengthy application process, he became part of the fight club that operated in the seedy underbelly of Mumbai.

Two weeks ago, Leo received an invitation to his first fight night which would take place later that night. The electronic invite told him when and where to be and provided a bar code he needed to bring. It didn't tell him anything about his opponent. Leo got off work early that afternoon and slept for a few hours. He took a cold shower and headed down to the lobby. He took a cab to the fight club venue not knowing what to expect when he got there.

It was a long cab ride to get to the venue. The cab driver pulled into a dimly lit street and stopped. "We are at the address you provided me, sir." The driver pointed to a five-story building covered in graffiti. He turned and looked at Leo and winked. "Have a good time, sir, and safety first!"

"What does that mean?" Leo wondered if the cab driver knew about the underground fight club.

"This is Kamathipura, also known as Lal Bazaar, the red-light district. There is only one reason people come here. Always use a condom sir." The cab driver chewed tobacco and spat out of the window. He flashed Leo a smile that showed his stained teeth.

Leo raised his voice. "That's not why I'm here." Leo's father paid for sex regularly, but he was nothing like his father. Leo paid the cab driver.

The cab driver frowned. "You come to a sex market and act like a saint," the cab driver mumbled in Marathi before speeding away.

Leo shook his head. He looked around the dimly lit street.

A street vendor sold food out of a brightly lit cart. "Food for energy, sir? Make you go long time." A speaker on the cart played a Bollywood song.

"No, thank you," said Leo.

People seated around the cart stuffed their faces and chatted loudly.

A little boy who looked seven or eight came up to Leo. "Hot chai, sir?" He carried tea holders containing six glasses of tea in each hand.

"Thanks. Maybe later," said Leo. The little boy worked late at night in a place where he shouldn't belong. "Take this." Leo handed the little boy a hundred-rupee bill.

The boy placed one of the tea holders on the ground and took the money. "Thank you, sir." He flashed Leo a toothless grin and tucked the bill into his underwear.

The putrid stench of garbage wafted to Leo's nostrils and made him gag. He covered his nose and looked around. The stench came from an overflowing dumpster in front of the building. Dogs fought over morsels they retrieved from the dumpster. Leo walked toward the entrance of the building.

"Want to have good time, baby?" Leo looked toward the source of the voice. Four women dressed provocatively stood on a balcony overlooking the street. "I give you best night," yelled one of the women. She then blew kisses at Leo and motioned for him to go over. Leo noticed that two of the women were young. "Baby, for your body, I give discount." One of the women sniggered.

Leo lowered his gaze.

The women giggled.

Leo felt pangs of sympathy and anger as he thought about women who were exploited and forced into the flesh trade.

Leo reached the building and walked to a desk where a man sat smoking a cigarette. The man was surrounded by a thick cloud of cigarette smoke.

Leo swatted the smoke away from his face. "I'm here for the fights." He took his phone out of his pocket and showed it to the man.

The man looked at the bar code on Leo's phone screen and took a drag. "Go over there." He pointed to a rusty iron door about twenty feet way.

Leo thanked the man and walked to the rusty door. He rang the doorbell.

A little compartment on the door opened and a man's face appeared. "What do you want?" The man yelled over music that blared in the background.

"I am one of the fighters tonight, and here is my bar code." Leo had to raise his voice to be heard. Leo held up his phone to the door.

The man squinted at the phone and motioned for Leo to wait. He disappeared and came back with a scanner. "Scan your code." The man held up the scanner and yelled.

Leo scanned his phone and the display on the scanner turned Green. The man closed the small compartment and opened the door. "Welcome to fight night." He grabbed a young boy's arm and pulled the boy close. "He will take you to the locker room."

"Follow me," said the boy. Leo followed the boy through a red door. The red door opened into a large room containing a hexagon fighting cage in the middle. "This is where the fights take place," the boy said, pointing to the cage.

"Hold on," said Leo. He looked around the large room. There was an eclectic mix of people in the room, people dressed in suits, shabbily dressed people, and people of different age groups and ethnicities. Their common factor was the blood lust in their eyes. A large bar covered one wall of the room and bartenders made drinks nonstop. Scantily clad women served drinks at the tables, whether by choice or not.

Leo followed the boy down a narrow hallway and reached the locker room. A few of the fighters had already arrived and were getting warmed up.

"Let me show you my special spot, in this locker room," the boy said. "Follow me." He took Leo to a dimly lit corner.

"Why is this your special spot, little man?" Leo set his duffel bag on the bench.

"I was dumped here as a baby. My mother found me three days after I was dumped. My biological mother was one of the working women from upstairs. My mother was the cleaning lady, and if she hadn't found me, I wouldn't be in this world. I call this my special spot because I was reborn here."

Leo frowned. "I'm sorry little man." He placed his hand on the boy's head. "I will be honored to use your special spot." The cruelty the little boy experienced was mindboggling. "Can you get me a bottle of water? I am going to get ready for the fight." Leo reached into his pocket and handed the little man a hundred-rupee bill.

"Thanks." The boy's eyes twinkled as he stuffed the money into a secret pocket inside his shirt sleeve. "Someday I want to go to school, and I am saving money for it," said the boy. "Yours is the second fight." The boy lowered his gaze and sighed.

"Why do you look worried?" Leo ruffled the boy's hair.

"The man you are fighting is dangerous and is known for hurting his opponents during fights." The boy pointed at a man.

Leo sized up his opponent. "Don't worry about me, little man." His opponent was about five and a half feet tall and well built. Leo was six foot one, and his long reach was going to be a huge advantage. Leo sat on the bench with his legs crossed and eyes closed and tuned out the noise around him. His mind and body balanced as his chi and chakras aligned.

The little boy came up to Leo. "It's almost time."

Leo put on his hand wraps and slipped on his fingerless mixed-martial-arts gloves. He followed the little man to the cage.

Leo's opponent was already in the hexagon, and from the reaction of the crowd, his opponent was the favorite. Leo got into the hexagon, and a few people clapped.

The announcer climbed into the ring. "All the way from Tel Aviv, Israel, Ex-Mossad, Israeli intelligence and special forces, and killing machine! Ladies and gentlemen, I present to you, the terror of Israel, Eitan." The crowd cheered as Leo's opponent raised both arms.

The announcer pointed at Leo. "Leonardo, the lion of India! First time fighter. Fresh meat." A few people in the audience clapped, while some shook their heads in sympathy. The little man stood outside the ring and whistled and clapped loudly.

Leo smiled at the little man.

The announcer stepped out of the ring and the referee came in. "Three rounds of four minutes each. When I blow the whistle, you stop. Understood?"

Leo and the Israeli bowed and went to their corners.

"Fight." The gong sounded, and the referee blew his whistle.

The Israeli went at Leo with incredible speed and threw various combinations. Leo was stuck in a corner and caught in a whirlwind of punches and kicks. The Israeli landed an elbow and gave Leo a gash over his left eyebrow. The crowd cheered as Leo felt the warmth of blood trickling down his face. The Israeli was trained in Krav Maga, a martial art technique developed in Israel. Leo was a black belt in Brazilian jiu-jitsu and decided to take down his opponent with wrestling moves. Leo swept the Israeli's foot and put him in a chokehold after the Israeli fell to the floor. The gong sounded, and the referee blew his whistle, signifying the end of the first round.

Leo retreated to his corner. The little man came to Leo's corner with petroleum jelly. He applied it on Leo's gash and stopped the bleeding. Leo ruffled the little man's hair and thanked him.

"Fight," said the referee. The second round was better for Leo. Leo ended the round with a hook, catching the Israeli square in the jaw, and followed it with a cross drawing blood from the Israeli's nose. The audience went crazy, barbarians who paid a lot of money to see blood spilled.

The Israeli came at Leo with everything in the third round. Leo managed to stand his ground, even though the Israeli landed multiple blows. The round was coming to an end and both fighters were exhausted. The Israeli threw a big hook, and Leo ducked under it. He swept the Israeli's foot and put him in an Achilles leg lock. "Tap out, man," shouted Leo as he heard the Israeli wince in pain. The referee blew the whistle and the Israeli was saved by the bell. He hobbled to Leo and extended his hand. Leo shook it and bowed in respect. The crowd cheered as the referee declared the Israeli the winner.

Soon, Leo had three fights under his belt. He had become fond of the little man and looked forward to meeting him later that night during his fourth fight.

Leo reached the venue and settled in the locker room. He got warmed up and wrapped his hands.

The little man came into the locker room. "Ready, champ?" the little man asked. "You are fighting a big guy today."

"Remember, the bigger they are, the harder they fall." Leo winked. "Listen, I am going to talk to your father today and ask him to put you in school. I am going to pay for you to go to school." Leo ruffled the little man's hair.

The little man's eyes lit up and then dropped. "I can't take money from you," said the little man.

"Consider it a loan. You can pay me back when you graduate and get a good job," said Leo with a smile.

The little man's eyes filled up. "Thank you, bhaiyya," said the little man, referring to Leo as his big brother.

Leo put on his gloves and meditated. He walked to the ring accompanied by the little man. "You weren't kidding about how big the guy is." Leo pegged the man at over seven feet tall. "I will be fine, little man." Leo saw the concern in his eyes. "After the fight we will talk to your dad about school."

The announcer introduced Leo's opponent as the Ukrainian giant. The Ukrainian landed combinations of knees, elbows, punches, and kicks all over Leo's body. By the third round, Leo was bloody and bruised. "Come on, big man. Is that all you got?" Leo moved around the ring and the Ukrainian followed slowly, exhausted. Leo ducked under the Ukrainian's cross and brought him to the ground with a kick to the liver. He put the Ukrainian in a jiu-jitsu knee bar and applied force on his left knee. The Ukrainian screamed in agony. "Tap out, big man," yelled Leo. He didn't want to rip out the Ukrainian's knee. The Ukrainian shrieked as his knee gave out. Leo had ripped the Ukrainian's cartilage and tendons, leaving his knee a soggy mess. Leo went up to the Ukrainian who writhed with agony. "I'm sorry big man."

The referee lifted Leo's arm. "Leonardo, the lion. The winner by technical knockout." The little man clapped hard and whistled. Leo chuckled and gave him the thumbs up.

Leo limped out of the locker room. He saw a man wearing a suit force the little man out of the door near the bar. "Stop," yelled Leo, hobbling to the bar. Leo flung the door open and saw a group of men wearing suits. One of the men held the little man by his neck. "Let him go! What do you want from him?" Leo put his duffel bag on the round.

The head of the Ukrainian gang stepped forward. "You beat my man in the fight today. He is the only fighter in my gang who hasn't lost a fight so far. Not anymore." The gangster puffed on his cigar. "The boy is not your business. Leave now."

Leo hobbled forward. "He is a child, please let him go."

The Ukrainian gangster shook his index finger. "He stole from me. Nobody steals from me. My brother left his cell phone in the bathroom and your little friend stole it."

Leo took out his wallet. "I will pay you. Please let him go."

"No one steals from me and lives to speak of it." The Ukrainian gangster looked at his man who held the little man and signaled. The Ukrainian shoved the little man into a white van.

Leo lunged forward. "Stop," he screamed. He felt a sharp pain in the back of his head and collapsed.

Leo opened his eyes and looked around. "Where am I?" He was on a bed in a dimly lit room.

A woman's voice startled Leo. "Welcome back." She came to the bed and sat by him.

"Who are you?" Leo clutched his throbbing head.

"I work in the building above the bar, and you are in my chambers." She handed Leo a cold compress.

"The boy?" Leo jumped out of the bed and rushed down the stairs to the bar. He searched frantically for the little man. "Where is the boy?" Leo asked the bartender.

The bartender motioned for Leo to meet him outside the door. Leo walked out the door, and the bartender followed. "The Ukrainian gangster took the kid." The bartender lit his cigarette and took a long drag. "He took the kid to Kiev as punishment for stealing his brother's cell phone." He took another drag and looked at Leo.

"How can he do that? What about the kid's father? He works here too. Why didn't he try to stop them?" Leo was furious.

"The father is a deadbeat, and he doesn't care for the kid. He is not the biological father, either. The father was paid to keep his mouth shut." The bartender took a long drag and threw the butt on the ground.

Leo's eyes blazed. "Do you know where the father lives?"

"I can get his address for you." The bartender went back to the bar.

***

Dharavi, a locality in Mumbai, known as one of the biggest slums in Asia, was a city within the city of Mumbai that housed hundreds of thousands of people. Home to tons of entrepreneurs who ran businesses, Dharavi generated revenues in the hundreds of millions of US dollars a year.

Leo walked into Dharavi cautiously. He had heard horror stories about being ambushed and mugged while inside. Instead, he came across ramshackle workshops and decrepit homes where hardworking people tried to build better lives for their families. He followed the instructions the bartender had given him and reached a three-foot-wide alley. He cupped his hand around his nose when the strong smell of sewage made him gag. The trash-strewn alley was covered with a layer of foul-smelling muck. Leo bought plastic bags and tied them around his shoes. He waded through the muck and stopped in front of a two-story hovel. The rickety structure was a jigsaw puzzle made of bricks, tin, and wood. A ladder that leaned on the side of the house granted access to the second floor.

Leo knocked on the door and a woman answered. "Who are you?" The woman asked in Marathi, the native language of Mumbai.

"I need to meet your husband, please," said Leo in broken Marathi.

"Wait here." She went inside and left the door open.

Leo peeked in and was surprised to see a large flat-screen TV, a branded refrigerator, and a kitchen with modern appliances. The interior of the house starkly contrasted with the exterior.

"Wake up," Leo heard the woman yell. "There is someone to see you."

"What is wrong with you, woman? Can't you see I am sleeping before going to work?" a man's voice yelled in Marathi.

"There is someone to see you." She pointed to the door.

The man put on a shirt and came to the door. He became shifty once he realized who Leo was. "What do you want?" The man avoided Leo's gaze.

"What happened last night? Where is your son?" Leo's eyes bore into the man.

"I have sent him to his uncle. He went to attend school." The man scratched his beard.

"Don't lie to me." Leo grabbed his neck.

The woman started crying.

"Do you know where you are?" the man yelled while waving his index finger in front of Leo's face. "This is Dharavi. If you touch one of us, you have declared war against us. You better leave now, or I'll call others and you won't leave here alive." The man's eyes were bloodshot.

"I don't want any trouble," said Leo. "I am trying to find out what happened to the little man." Leo let go of the man's neck.

"I told you he is with his uncle." The man raised his voice. "I am his father and I will decide what is best for him. Leave. Make me food," the man turned to his wife and yelled. "I need to go to work." He shut the door in Leo's face.

Leo decided to follow the man and confront him outside Dharavi. Leo's olfactory sensors became numb and the smell of sewage didn't bother him on his walk back. He grabbed his hat and sunglasses and waited for the little man's father to come out of his house.

After a short while, the little man's father came out of the alley wearing pants and a shirt. Leo followed the man out of Dharavi keeping a safe distance. The man walked for a while and turned into a dingy alley. He walked to the end of the alley and entered a door. Leo entered the door and found himself in a hole-in-the-wall bar and restaurant. Cigarette smoke filled the place and Bollywood music blared.

Leo sat at the bar and looked around. He saw the little man's father serve food and drinks. "What can I get you?" The bartender asked in Hindi.

"Beer, please," said Leo.

"Hundred and sixty rupees or if you are paying in American, it's two dollars and fifteen cents," said the bartender. He placed a chilled bottle of beer in front of Leo.

Leo chuckled. "Rupees it is. Keep the change." Leo handed the bartender two hundred rupees.

"Thanks, sir," said the bartender, overjoyed at the generous tip.

"What can you tell me about him?" Leo pointed at the little man's father.

The bartender yelled over the loud music. "He does odd jobs sir. He works here a couple of times a week. A real piece of work."

"When does his shift get over today?" Leo took a large swig of his cold beer.

"He wraps up at nine tonight," said the bartender. "Anything else, sir?" Leo shook his head. He finished his beer and walked out of the bar reeking of cigarette smoke.

Leo came back to the alley at 8.45 when it was dark. He hid behind a dumpster and waited. The little man's father came out of the bar a little after nine and lit a cigarette. Leo sneaked up behind him and held a steel pipe against his back. "If you make noise, I will empty my gun into your back."

The man trembled. "Who are you? What do you want from me?"

"Keep walking and I will tell you." Leo took him to the end of the alley, which was dark and deserted. "Where is your son?" Leo turned him around and grabbed his throat. "Where is he?" Leo choked him. "I want the truth."

The little man's father gasped for air. "I will tell you the truth. Please let me go." Leo relaxed his hold, and the man took deep breaths. "The Ukrainian gangster took him to Kiev and told me if I tried to stop him, he would kill me and the rest of my family."

"You are his father, you were supposed to protect him." Leo grunted as he tightened his grip.

"I am not his father. My wife found him in the bar. He had been dumped by his prostitute mother." The man choked. "The Ukrainian paid me well for him."

Rage consumed Leo and he punched the man over and over. He stopped once the man's face became a bloody mess. "I should kill you for what you have done." Leo threw him on the ground like a rag doll and walked away feeling hopeless. He knew he would never see the little man again.

Leo stood on his balcony and stared at the ocean that sparkled under the starry sky.

A voice caught him off guard. "Hey, neighbor." He turned to his left to see a woman standing on the balcony next to his. Her green eyes sparkled, and her hair was pulled back into a messy bun held together by a pencil. "I'm Isabella, Isa. I just moved in." She raised a bottle of water. "How are you doing?"

"Hey, Isa, I'm Leo. I've been living here for a while. I've had a rough day." Leo sipped on his beer.

"Want to talk about it?" Isa sounded genuine.

Leo confided in her. He felt his burden lighten after talking to her.

"Good night Leo. I hope you find peace and overcome the darkness." She headed into her apartment.

Leo, who was living life one day at a time, experienced a cathartic moment. He wept before gaining composure. Losing the little man showed Leo the path he was going to take. He couldn't protect the little man, but he was going to hunt and punish criminals who preyed on the innocent.

CHAPTER THREE

WOLF IN SHEEP'S CLOTHING

Mumbai, October 2016

Leo stood in his favorite spot in Mumbai, his balcony that overlooked the ocean. He was lost in his thoughts while he stared into the ocean that glistened under the starry night.

Leo was startled by Isa's voice. "This is a beautiful spot."

"Hey, Isa. It's my little happy corner." Leo sipped on his beer. "How is Mumbai treating you?" He turned to face Isa.

"It is an enchanting city." The ocean breeze blew her hair back. "I am falling in love with it." Isa brushed a few strands of hair off her face.

"Is it different from your hometown Kolkata?

A sudden gust of wind caused Isa's loose-fitting shirt to hug her curves.

Leo caught a glimpse of Isa's toned body. He quickly looked away, because he didn't want to make her uncomfortable. "Can I get you a beer? I would love to hear about your life before you came here and your hometown."

Isa smiled. "I will have a beer and would love to tell you my story. I will get some snacks to go with the beer," said Isa.

"Are you twenty-one, Isa? I don't want to serve alcohol to a minor."
Leo shrugged. "In Mumbai you have to be twenty-one to drink beer
and twenty-three to drink wine or hard liquor."

"As flattering as that is, I am not going to tell you my age, Leo. I am
old enough to drink beer." Isa shook her head and walked into her
apartment.

Leo came back with a cooler full of beer on ice and placed it on the
balcony floor.

Isa placed a bowl of mixture, a spicy crispy snack, and a bowl of
potato chips on their shared balcony wall.

"Looks delicious." Leo opened a bottle of beer and handed it to Isa.

"Cheers. To neighbors." Isa raised her glass.

"To neighbors I don't hate." Leo raised his glass. "Tell me who Isa is
and how she ended up in Mumbai."

Isa met Leo's gaze. "I will start with my parents, opposites who were
brought together by fate." Isa took a sip of the cold beer. "My father
was an introverted electrical engineering student at the prestigious
Kolkata Technology Institute. He lived with his parents in a small
apartment on the bank of the Hooghly River. His world consisted
of his parents, his college, and poetry. He spent time whenever he
could on the banks of the river and wrote poetry. My mother, on the
other hand, was a socialite and was born into a wealthy family."

"Opposites attract," said Leo as he wondered whether she got her
good looks from her mother or her father. "The mixture is delicious.
The spicy and tangy flavors go well with the beer." Leo put another
spoonful of mixture into his mouth. "Continue."

Isa ate a potato chip. "One night my father was sitting on the
riverbank when he heard the screech of car tires a few feet above
him, on the road. He saw something roll down the slope and land a

short distance from him in the river. The car sped away. He ran to the object and was shocked to see that it was a woman. He pulled her out of the water and checked her pulse. He gave her CPR, and she woke up coughing." Isa took another sip of her beer.

"Was she okay? Who were the people in the car?" asked Leo with eyebrows raised and arched.

"My mother took drugs with her friends on her way to a party. Her friends panicked when she was unresponsive and pushed her into the river. My dad saved her life. He took care of her and took her home in his parents' car." Isa took a deep breath.

"Your dad, the hero." Leo raised his bottle. "Respect."

Isa lifted her bottle in acknowledgment. "A few days later my dad was working on assignments in the university library when he heard a group of students making a lot of noise. He got angry because he was trying to focus, but then he recognized my mother sitting in the group. My mom went over and asked him out. That's how my dad went on the first date of his life." Isa pulled a few strands of hair off her face.

Leo caught Isa's gaze. "Do you look like your mom or your dad?"

Isa's green eyes twinkled. "People tell me that I am the spitting image of my mother."

Leo turned to face Isa. "Well Isa, I will say your mom was a beautiful woman."

Isa blushed. "My mom was beautiful, and you are a flirt."

Leo felt drawn to Isa and her infectious smile.

Isa put her beer bottle on the balcony wall. "My dad and mom were dating, and before they knew it, graduation time was upon them. Neither of them had told their parents about each other because they belonged to different religions and different social classes.

Both sets of my grandparents didn't agree to their union. My mom's parents disowned her when she told them she wanted to marry a Hindu man instead of a Christian man. My parents decided to leave home and start their married lives in New Delhi. Two years later, I was born. The only person who maintained a relationship with my parents was my paternal grandmother." Isa sighed.

Leo shook his head. "I still don't understand how people can put religion before family."

Isa shrugged. "I was ten years old when my parents left me at our neighbor's house and attended a work event hosted by my father's company. I remember how excited my parents were, because my dad was getting a promotion at work. While they were driving back home later that night, a truck crashed into their little car and threw it fifteen feet into a quarry. It caught on fire. Both my parents were pronounced dead at the scene." Isa teared up and bit her trembling lip.

Leo put both his hands up. "I am really sorry, Isa. I didn't mean to open old wounds."

Isa wiped her tears. "I'm okay. It's been many years since it happened. I haven't told this story to anyone in a very long time. My paternal grandparents raised me from that point. I finished my undergraduate degree in architecture in Kolkata. My true passion is music, and I play the violin and the cello. I got admitted to an arts and music program, and that's what brought me to Mumbai. That's my story, and that is who Isa is." She finished her beer.

Leo cracked open another one and handed it to her. "You will have to play something for me someday Isa. I am glad you came to Mumbai." Leo grinned sheepishly.

Isa laughed. "Thanks. I am glad I came to Mumbai too."

***

Isa's scholarship paid for her master's program. She received a healthy monthly stipend that took care of her living expenses. In addition, she gave violin and cello lessons to kids on weekday evenings.

One evening Isa got ready for her children's violin classes in the college auditorium. She had six students that evening and among them was Arya, a gifted violinist. At the end of the group session, Isa would give Arya a one-on-one session.

The group session ended and everyone except Arya packed their violins.

Isa put her violin in its case. "Thank you, class, I will see you all day after tomorrow. Great work today." The students took their instruments and left the auditorium.

Twelve-year-old Arya stayed back and waited in her seat.

Isa walked to Arya. "You ready Arya?"

Arya smiled enthusiastically.

Arya had a high intelligence quotient and Isa tried to develop her emotional quotient. Isa challenged Arya to expand her horizon.

Isa placed a book on a stand in front of Arya. "Arya, the page I have left open on the book is from Vivaldi's "Four Seasons". Go ahead and play it."

Arya placed her violin under her chin. She closed her eyes and took a deep breath. She opened her eyes and began playing.

A man wearing a suit walked into the auditorium and interrupted Arya's session. "That was beautiful baby."

Isa jumped up from her chair. "I'm sorry, you are not supposed to be in here. I'm going to call security."

The man extended his hand and walked toward Isa. "I'm sorry, I didn't mean to startle you. I am Arya's father, Raj Sinha."

Isa shook his hand. "Oh, sorry. Nice to meet you, Mr. Sinha. I'm Isabella, Isa."

"Raj, you can call me Raj. I am sorry to interrupt the session, but I will need to take my daughter home early today. She will be back to class next week."

Arya packed up her violin. "Dad, I need to use the restroom." She walked to the restroom in the corner.

Sinha moved closer to Isa. "Isa, I would like to invite you to Arya's thirteenth birthday party this weekend. She talks a lot about you, and it would be great if you can make it," said Sinha.

Isa smiled. "Thank you. I would like that. What time is the party?" Isa asked.

Sinha took out his phone. "It's on Saturday around noon. I will send a car to pick you up. Give me your address."

Isa didn't like how forward Sinha was with her. "That won't be necessary. I'll take a cab."

"Works for me." Sinha handed Isa his address as Arya came back. "It was nice meeting you" said Sinha.

Arya waved goodbye and left with her father.

***

Isa got ready on the day of Arya's birthday party and called a cab. She took the elevator down and got into the taxi.

The cab driver turned to face Isa. "Good morning madam, it's about a twenty-minute drive to the address you provided." The young driver put the car in gear.

Isa had made Arya a CD with violin pieces from Chopin, Vivaldi, Bach, and Beethoven. She had become attached to Arya and looked forward to celebrating Arya becoming a teenager.

The cab driver pulled up in front of a large gate. "We are here, madam."

"Thank you," said Isa as she got out of the cab. She walked to the watchman who stood in front of the gate. The cab sped away.

Isa stopped in front of the watchman. "Hello, I am here for Arya's birthday party."

The watchman saluted and opened the gate. "Welcome, madam, please go this way."

Isa looked around. "Where are the other guests?" She asked the watchman.

Before the watchman could answer, a voice called out to Isa. "Welcome Isa madam, you are the first guest to arrive for Arya baby's birthday. All others are fashionably late as always." A woman wearing a red sari and tons of makeup came up to Isa. Her mouth was red from the betel leaves she chewed on. "Please have some juice and have a seat. Someone will come and escort you to the party." She handed Isa a glass of cold pineapple juice.

"Thank you," said Isa as she took the glass from the woman. The cold juice was a welcome reprieve from the terrible humidity in Mumbai. Isa sat down on a plush leather sofa and sipped on the juice. After she finished the juice, Isa felt weak and the room started to spin. The last thing she saw before she passed out was the amused face of the woman who had given her the juice.

When Isa woke up, she was on a bed and didn't have any clothes on. She tried to sit up but felt weak. She stumbled out of the bed and found her clothes on the floor. She tried to compose herself and figure out what was going on.

The woman in red appeared. "How are you feeling? I hope you are feeling as good as Mr. Sinha." The woman continued to chew on betel leaves.

Isa grabbed her pulsing forehead. "The last thing I remember is drinking the juice you gave me. What happened? Why am I on the bed naked?" Isa managed to put on her clothes and sit on the bed.

The woman cackled. "You and Mr. Sinha had a good time on the bed."

"What are you talking about?" yelled Isa. She felt drained.

"You and Mr. Sinha had sex on the bed. I have never seen Mr. Sinha so happy. He enjoyed himself." The woman laughed maniacally. "There were many before, but you are something special."

Isa felt broken when she realized what happened. "He raped me! I will have him thrown in jail. He will be punished." She got up from the bed and stumbled to the woman.

The woman took a step back. "There is no evidence of rape. I bathed you and all evidence has been removed. There is no evidence of a struggle, and you don't have any bruises or marks on your body. Mr. Sinha has been kind to you and left you a good amount of money." The lady pointed to the table by the bed. "Seems like he enjoyed himself quite a bit. I haven't seen him pay that high before. Take the money and forget this ever happened. It's not like you remember anything anyway."

"Where is my phone?" Isa screamed.

The woman put betel leaves in her mouth. "Once you get dressed and go to the gate, the security guard will give it to you." The woman motioned for her to leave.

Isa stumbled out of the room. "Tell Sinha this is the last time he will ever do this to anyone. I will destroy him."

The woman escorted Isa to the gate. The watchman handed Isa her purse.

As Isa stumbled down the road, she saw a cab and waved it down. She got in with tears streaming down her face. "Please take me to the nearest police station," she told the cab driver. She buried her face in her palms and cried.

The driver looking at Isa through the rearview mirror. "Are you okay, madam?"

She wiped her tears and looked determined. "I need to get to the nearest police station. I was raped."

The driver clenched his jaw. "We will be at the police station in fifteen minutes. Madam, please make sure to remember all the details, because you will need to tell them exactly what happened. If there are any discrepancies in your statement, it will be held against you in court."

Isa stared at the driver. Even though she was disoriented, she asked. "How do you know these things?"

The cab driver caught Isa's stare in the rearview mirror. "I am a law student. I am helping my sick father by driving his cab for a few days," the cab driver said.

A short drive later the cab came to a halt. The driver turned to face Isa. "We are here, madam. Remember, it will be uncomfortable, but provide all the details. I hope the bastard rots in hell." He handed Isa a piece of paper. "In case you need me in court, madam, here are my phone number and license plate number."

Isa paid the driver. "I appreciate your help." She stepped out of the car. She took a deep breath and walked into the police station.

Isa reached the police constable desk. "I need to file a complaint," said Isa.

The constable pointed to a chair. "Please have a seat, madam. What do you want to file a complaint about?" The constable took out a sheet of paper from a drawer in his desk.

Isa sat down. "I was raped." She didn't break eye contact.

The constable jumped out of his chair. "Please wait here, madam." He hurried into an office through swinging half doors.

He came back out shortly. "You can go into the office, and the inspector will take your complaint madam." He gestured to the swinging doors.

Isa thanked the constable. She could feel the gazes of people follow her as she walked into the office. She was relieved to see a female police officer when she entered. "Come in and have a seat. What is your name?" The inspector pointed to a chair across from her.

"Isa, Isabella Basu." Isa sat on the chair.

"I understand you would like to file rape charges. Is that accurate?" The inspector's voice was compassionate yet assertive.

"I was raped this afternoon, and I want the animal who did this to me to rot in jail." Isa felt the urge to break down, but she took a deep breath and stayed strong.

"Isa, you did the right thing by coming here. A lot of perpetrators escape because rape victims are reluctant to come forward and report these heinous crimes." The inspector picked up the phone and talked to someone in Marathi. "I have called the local counselor who works with us on rape cases, and she will be here shortly. Once she gets here, we will head to the government facility and have a rape kit done. Don't worry, Isa, we will do our best to punish the scum who did this to you."

Isa felt strong and confident after talking to the inspector.

Shortly, an older woman walked into the inspector's office and introduced herself as the counselor. "Isa, I am really sorry you went through such a traumatic experience. Let's go," the counselor said with a sense of urgency. "We need to get there as soon as possible so we can collect evidence and build our case."

The inspector got up and put on her police cap. "Let's take the next step to getting you justice, Isa." She walked out of the swinging doors, and Isa followed her. The police jeep pulled up in front of the station and the inspector got in the front. Isa and the counselor got in the back.

A short ride later, the jeep pulled up in front of the government hospital. "Follow me, Isa." The inspector jumped out and walked up steps leading into the building.

The three women walked down a hallway and reached a door with a forensic lab sign on top. The inspector knocked on the door, and it was opened by a middle-aged woman.

The woman grinned and hugged the inspector. "Well, well, well, if it isn't the protector of Mumbai."

"Unfortunately, this isn't a pleasant situation. We have a rape victim, and I need to get a rape kit done." The inspector urged Isa to step forward.

The woman stopped grinning and looked at Isa with compassion. "Come in, child. I am a state-certified gynecologist and will perform your rape kit today. I am really sorry you had to endure such cruelty." She took Isa's arm and walked her into the lab.

The counselor took a seat inside the lab and the inspector followed. "You are in good hands Isa. The inspector and I will wait here for you."

The gynecologist pointed to the bed. "Put on the gown that's on the bed and put your clothes into the plastic bag. I'll be back shortly." She stepped out of the room and closed the door behind her.

When she came back, Isa had on the gown and her clothes were in the plastic bag.

The gynecologist put her arm on Isa's shoulder. "I have a tape recorder and a notepad, and I will make my notes based on the information you provide." She held up the recorder and the notepad. "Please lie down on the examination table."

Isa complied.

The gynecologist put on latex gloves. "This is going to feel a little uncomfortable, but it is vital for the case we are going to build."

The doctor started her examination and Isa turned her head away and tried to escape to a happy place. The doctor collected all the necessary samples for the rape kit.

The gynecologist disposed her gloves. "We are done with the kit, Isa, you may sit up. I will call the inspector and counselor, and you will need to give your statement. You did great. This is an important step to punish the criminal." The doctor held Isa's hand.

Isa sat up. "I won't be at peace until he is punished," Isa said with determination in her voice.

"I hope it won't be too long, Isa." The gynecologist went out of the room and came back with the inspector and the counselor.

The inspector pulled up a chair and sat down by the examination table. "Isa, I need you to walk me through the events that transpired today and the events the led up to today's events."

Isa went through the details, and the inspector captured them. "I have everything I need to file the FIR against Sinha. We will take him into custody once we have enough evidence to charge him. Isa, you are brave." The inspector stood up and thanked the gynecologist.

The counselor handed Isa her business card. "Isa, in case you feel the need to talk about what happened today, I want you to know I am here for you." The counselor took Isa's hand in hers.

"Thank you," said Isa. "You all have already helped me so much and I feel optimistic I will get justice." Isa got down from the examination table.

"Would you like me to drop you home Isa?" the inspector asked Isa.

"If you don't mind, I'm exhausted," said Isa.

The gynecologist came to Isa. "Here is a change of clothes. It's not fashionable by any means." The gynecologist handed her a new plain cotton Salwar Kameez, a traditional outfit worn by Indian women. "We keep a few of these on hand for situations like yours. It's loose fitting and plain, and it will work much better than a hospital gown. Take care, and I wish you all the best in court. I have a lot of faith in the inspector, and she will nail the bastard."

Isa changed into the Salwar Kameez and came out of the room where the inspector waited for her.

"Ready?" the inspector asked.

Isa nodded. Isa and the inspector went out of the hospital and got into the police jeep.

The inspector turned to Isa. "Get a good night's rest Isa. Tomorrow, we will meet the public prosecutor who will represent your case against Sinha. I know this is the worst thing that could happen to a woman, but stay strong, and we will do everything in our power to get justice."

The jeep pulled in front of Isa's apartment building. "Thanks for everything, inspector," said Isa. "I am not afraid to look Sinha in the eye and call him out for what he is. I will be ready tomorrow." A fire of determination and hope blazed in Isa's eyes. "Justice will prevail."

"You are a strong woman, Isa. We need more women like you in this world." The inspector tapped her hand twice on the dashboard, and the driver put the jeep in gear and drove away.

As the police jeep pulled in, Leo was driving out of the apartment complex. He saw Isa in the jeep and parked his car and jumped out. He rushed toward Isa as the police jeep drove past him. "What happened, Isa? Are you okay?"

Isa stared at Leo without saying anything.

"Isa?" Leo's voice was louder.

"I was raped." Isa trembled.

Leo clenched his fists. "What?" Rage engulfed Leo. His face turned red and his body shivered. The only time he had felt such rage were on his twenty first birthday, and when the little man was taken. "Who did this to you, Isa?" Leo had visions of ripping out the rapist's limbs.

Isa lowered her gaze. "It was the father of one of my students. I can't talk right now, Leo. I need some space." Isa looked subdued and distant.

"I am here for you. Anything you need me to do, let me know," said Leo.

Isa lowered her gaze and walked into the apartment building.

Leo felt murderous and needed to calm his mind. He canceled his training sessions at the gym and headed to Marine Drive. He ran for two hours while listening to classical music. The run cleansed his mind and body of destructive emotions, and he returned to his normal state of mind. The events that transpired solidified Leo's intentions of dedicating his life to taking down criminals.

CHAPTER FOUR

JUSTICE IS BLIND

Mumbai, January 2017

Isa tossed and turned on her bed until she finally fell asleep. She was awakened by her alarm early the next morning. It was going to be an important morning for Isa, because she was meeting the prosecutor handling her case. Isa got dressed and took a cab to the prosecutor's office.

She was welcomed by a young woman in a suit. "Good morning, my name is Kajal, and I will be handling your case on behalf of prosecution. Come into my office." Kajal was only twenty-eight years old and the youngest prosecutor in Mumbai.

"Good morning, Kajal. Thanks for helping me out." Isa was pleasantly surprised to see that her case would be handled by a female lawyer. She followed Kajal into her office.

"Good morning, Isa." The familiar voice of the inspector called out to Isa.

"Good morning. I'm really glad to see you here." Isa felt more at ease when she saw the inspector in Kajal's office.

"I am personally handling your case. I arrested Sinha on the charges of rape early this morning. Thought you would like to know that." The inspector beamed.

"That's great news. Is the bastard in jail?" Isa was ecstatic to hear that Sinha had been arrested.

"Unfortunately, not, said Kajal. He is in a holding cell and will make bail tomorrow, more than likely. Sinha and his legal team will plead not guilty and request bail at the preliminary hearing." Kajal pulled out the police report from a file on her desk. "Tomorrow the judge will either agree or disagree to Sinha's bail and then set the date for the trial."

Isa looked at the file.

Kajal held up the inspector's report. "Let's go over your report. I want you to go through all the details. I want to make sure there are no discrepancies. If there are, we will lose credibility, and it will be held against us."

Isa went through the events in detail until Kajal was satisfied. "I'm not going to sugar coat this. It's going to be a tough case. It's your word against Sinha's. The important points are that we can place you at the scene of the crime and there were traces of drugs found in your system." Kajal closed the file.

Isa opened her purse. "I have the contact information for the cab driver who brought me to the police station after the incident. He is a law student and told me that he would be glad to come to court and testify if needed." Isa handed Kajal the piece of paper containing the cab driver's contact information.

Kajal took the piece of paper. "Good. It can't hurt to have someone credible on the stand. I will see you in court at nine tomorrow morning. We are going to have long and arduous days ahead while we get ready for the trial. Hang in there, we will do our best." Kajal held out her hand and Isa shook it.

Isa got up from her chair. "Will you be in court tomorrow inspector?"

The inspector put on her cap. "Wouldn't miss it. Also, I want you to know that I dragged Sinha out of his house this morning in handcuffs. I made sure all his neighbors and his family saw us arresting him and shoving him in the jeep." The inspector stood up and hugged Isa.

Isa took a leave of absence from school for a few weeks. She was going to stay home and recover from the trauma she had experienced.

Isa reached the courthouse a few minutes early the next morning. She waited on a bench outside the courthouse. She was anxious at the thought of facing Sinha.

Kajal came up to Isa dressed in her advocate's gown. "You ready?" Power and confidence radiated from Kajal.

"I was born ready," said Isa. Isa tried to use humor to hide her nervousness.

Kajal chuckled. "That's my girl. Let's go look the predator in the eye and tell him that we are going to take him down."

Kajal and Isa took their seats in the courtroom and waited for the judge and the Sinha's defense team to arrive.

A well-groomed older man walked into the courtroom followed by two younger men. They set down their paperwork.

The older man walked up to Kajal. "Kajal, can I have a moment please?" The man walked up to the judge's desk and stopped.

Kajal followed the man. She stopped in front of him and folded her arms across her chest. "What is the going price for selling one's soul these days?"

The older man chuckled. "I see you still have your sense of humor. Look, Kajal, if you drop the charges, we can save your client the embarrassment of going through the trial. You know very well that there is no compelling evidence against my client. She looks like a nice girl." The man looked toward Isa.

Kajal took her time before answering. "If your teenage daughter came home and told you that someone drugged and raped her, would you be having the same conversation?" Kajal's eyes bore into the man's eyes.

"Don't you dare bring my daughter into this!" He waved his finger in front of Kajal.

Kajal didn't flinch. "This nice girl is actually a strong woman. You do your job, and let me do mine. I am going to go for the maximum penalty." Kajal turned and walked back to her seat.

"What happened?" asked Isa anxiously. "Who is that man?"

Kajal sat down next to Isa. "He is a highly paid hot-shot lawyer who represents wealthy and powerful people. His clientele are politicians, business tycoons, and celebrities. We are up against Goliath." Kajal placed her hand on Isa's and gave it a squeeze. "We'll do our best."

The bailiff stood up. "All rise. The honorable judge is here"

The judge sat down. "Please be seated," said the judge. He opened the file on his desk. "Today is the arraignment in the case of the state versus Mr. Raj Sinha. Defendant, how do you plead in the case of the rape of Miss. Isabella Basu?" The judge looked at Sinha.

"Not guilty, your honor," said Sinha "I haven't-"

Before he could complete his sentence, his lawyer grabbed his arm and told him to be silent. "Your honor, Mr. Sinha is an esteemed member of society and has a wife and two young daughters. We would like to request bail and are willing to surrender his passport, his government ID, and his driver's license." Sinha's lawyer looked expectantly at the judge.

Kajal jumped in. "Given the heinous nature of the crime, your honor, I request that bail be denied."

"Innocent until proven guilty," said Sinha's lawyer looking at Kajal.

"Ms. Kajal, even though the crime is heinous, defense is right. Mr. Sinha is innocent until proven guilty. Bail is set at two million rupees. The hearing will be in six days. The court is adjourned." The judge struck his gavel against the sound block on his table and walked out of the court room.

Isa felt Sinha's filthy gaze as he walked out of the courtroom. .

Kajal placed her hand on Isa's shoulder. "We got to prepare well for next week. Don't worry about today. Let's work towards next week." She got up and left the courtroom.

Isa felt dejected, but she was going to fight hard.

***

Leo stood on his balcony one evening when he was pleasantly surprised by Isa's voice. She hadn't been on the balcony since her incident with Sinha. Leo worried about Isa and missed their conversations. "Couldn't sleep," said Isa. She stood facing the ocean.

"Me either. How are you holding up?" said Leo.

"I'm afraid. Tomorrow is the court hearing, and there is a good chance that Sinha will walk away." She had lost the sparkle in her eyes, and it pained Leo to see her that way.

"I would like to be with you in court tomorrow. If you are comfortable with that," said Leo.

"You have been a good friend, Leo. I would like that. I can use all the support I can get," said Isa with a forced smile.

Leo drove Isa to court the next morning. They reached the court-house twenty minutes before the scheduled trial start time. Kajal and the inspector arrived shortly. Kajal and Isa took their seats at the counsel table, and Leo took a seat in the first row of the gallery behind them.

"I am going to the bathroom. Be back shortly." Leo got up and walked out of the courtroom.

Leo opened the bathroom door. A man dressed in an expensive suit washed his hands. Leo recognized the man. He was the same man who stood with the Ukrainian gangster the night the little man was kidnapped.

Leo felt hopeful about getting a lead on the little man's disappearance. "Excuse me sir," said Leo. "I remember you from a few months ago, when you had attended a fight night in Kamathipura," said Leo.

The man turned off the faucet. "Ah, yes, I do remember attending the fight night. It was entertaining." He dried his hands as he looked at Leo. "Did you attend too?"

"I was one of the fighters that night," said Leo.

The man in the suit waved his finger in front of Leo with a big smile. "Ah, I remember you now. You ripped out the Ukrainian fighter's knee. It was the best thing I ever saw." He laughed maniacally.

Leo forced a smile. "I asked him to tap out, but he wouldn't. I wanted to ask you about the Ukrainian gangster. That night after the fights, you were standing with the Ukrainian gangster when they kidnapped a little boy. I just want to find out how I can get to the boy. Can you help me?" Leo did his best to stay composed.

The man stared at Leo. "You were the one who burst out of the door that night asking the Ukrainian to let the boy go. They knocked you out. You were lucky they didn't kill you." The man in the suit looked in the mirror and straightened his tie. "Look, I met the Ukrainian for the first time that night. He was introduced to me as a potential business contact, but I haven't heard from him since that night.

Either way, the kid probably died a painful death." The man combed his hair and turned to face Leo. "I would love to stay and chat, but I have a rape case against me that I need to win." He turned to the bathroom door.

Leo turned red with rage when he realized that the man in the suit was Sinha, Isa's rapist. He was about to lunge forward and grab Sinha by the neck when the bathroom door opened, and two police constables came in. "Time for the trial, sir. We need to go." The constables escorted Sinha out of the bathroom.

Leo washed his face a few times and calmed himself before heading back to the courtroom.

"All rise. The honorable judge is in chambers," said the bailiff. Everyone in the courtroom stood up.

The judge walked in. "Please have a seat. Are both prosecution and defense ready? Let's keep it respectful and clean in my court." The judge looked at both sides. "Prosecution may call its first witness."

Kajal called the government gynecologist to the stand and she was sworn in. "Doctor, can you please describe the findings of your tests on Ms. Basu?"

Everyone in the room looked at the doctor.

The doctor looked at the judge. "I found traces of GHB, a date-rape drug in Ms. Basu's system. I also found bruising consistent with penetration." She glared at Sinha.

Kajal walked up to the witness box. "Based on your expertise, would you agree that Ms. Basu was raped?"

"Objection," yelled Sinha's lawyer. "The doctor's opinion without proof means nothing." He threw his arms up in the air.

"Overruled," said the judge. "Please answer the question."

The gynecologist paused for a moment before answering. "Based on my extensive experience with rape victims, Miss. Basu's testimony and her physical condition were consistent with someone who was raped." The doctor kept her gaze locked with Kajal. "Sinha raped her."

"Come on," shouted Sinha's lawyer.

The judge gave the doctor a stern look. "I will disregard that statement. You know better than that doctor."

"No further questions." Kajal retreated to her seat.

"Your witness," the judge told Sinha's lawyer.

Sinha's lawyer approached the witness stand. "Doctor, would it be possible to get the same results if Ms. Basu had consumed a large amount of GHB recreationally the previous night and had sexual intercourse with someone? Would that scenario present the same results?" Sinha's lawyer looked intimidating.

"The drug doesn't stay in the system for very long. She had to have taken it in the morning." The doctor refused to look Sinha's lawyer in the face.

"Doctor, that was a yes or no question. We don't need you to beat around the bush." Sinha's lawyer slammed his palm on the witness stand.

"Yes, it's possible." The doctor clenched her jaw.

"Did you find any DNA evidence linking my client to the heinous crime he is being accused of?" Sinha's lawyer pointed at Sinha.

"Unfortunately, she had been given a bath in the accused's house. This took away any traces of DNA." The doctor shifted in her seat.

"Doctor, once again, that was a yes or no question. Please stick to answering the question instead of sharing your opinion." Sinha's lawyer looked at the judge, exasperated.

"Please answer the question doctor," the judge said.

"No, I didn't." The doctor's eyes were bloodshot.

"No more questions." Sinha's lawyer retreated to his seat.

"You are excused, doctor. Thank you for your exemplary work," said the judge.

Kajal called Sinha to the stand next. "Two years ago, a woman filed a complaint against you for rape. This is not your first time, is it? Seems like you like drugging and raping young women." Kajal went up to the witness box and got in Sinha's face.

"Objection," yelled Sinha's lawyer. "The attorney is testifying, and the information is not relevant."

"Sustained," said the judge. "Ms. Kajal. No personal attacks. please. Stick to the case."

"Seems like you are a man who is sexually inept. Maybe a biological problem with size and no one will voluntarily have sex with you." Kajal pushed Sinha's buttons to try and get a reaction, and it worked.

Before Sinha's lawyer could object, Sinha jumped up. "I don't have a small penis. I would love to show it to you one day."

Sinha's lawyer facepalmed.

Kajal walked up to Sinha and stared him in the eye. "Would you need to drug me and incapacitate me before showing me your penis?"

"Shut up, you bitch," screamed Sinha turning red.

"Sit down, Mr. Sinha," the judge shouted. "I will hold you in contempt of court."

Sinha sat down quietly.

"Ms. Kajal, this is your last warning. If you pull another stunt like that, I will take you off the case," said the judge.

Kajal put her palms up. "Sorry, judge. Just trying to expose the character of the accused." Kajal turned to Isa. "Did you see Miss. Basu on the day of your daughter's birthday party?" Kajal pointed toward Isa.

"I didn't," said Sinha. My staff told me later that she was sick when she came in and they took care of her. Once she felt better, she left."

"Why didn't you check on her? You had invited her personally. Or did you rape her and have your staff clean up your mess?" Kajal pushed Sinha.

"Objection," said Sinha's lawyer. "This is a personal attack on my client."

"I agree. One more incident, Ms. Agarwal, and you are done." The judge waved his index finger at Kajal.

"Were you at your daughter's birthday party the whole time?" Kajal stood right in front of the witness box and glared at Sinha.

"I went between the party and doing paperwork in my study." Sinha was prepared. "This is absurd, your honor," said Sinha's lawyer. "These antics are designed to disorient my client. I think he has been through enough already. Request that he be excused."

"No more questions," said Kajal.

"You are excused, Mr. Sinha." The judge motioned for Sinha to leave.

Sinha's defense called the watchman on duty and the woman who had given Isa the laced juice at Sinha's house. Both swore under oath that Isa was sick when she arrived at Sinha's house. The woman said that she took care of Isa and let her sleep for a few hours and that Isa then woke up and left.

Kajal's closing statement was powerful and thought provoking. It told the story of a young and innocent woman who had been preyed on by a rich and powerful man.

Sinha's lawyer labeled Isa as an unstable drug user. He said that Isa was already on drugs when she came into Sinha's house. Once she realized that Sinha was rich, she had concocted a story and was hoping for financial gain. He painted Sinha to be the ideal father and husband and a cornerstone of society.

"Thank you for presenting both sides of the story. The court will take a one-hour recess and I will announce the verdict when we reconvene." The judge stood up and went to his chambers.

The hour was excruciating for Isa. She waited with bated breath.

The judge walked into the courtroom after the recess. "Please be seated. Rape is on the rise in our country. We have amended our laws to ensure that anyone who is convicted of rape will not receive any form of leniency. After carefully reviewing the evidence presented by both sides in this case, I have reached a verdict. Due to lack of evidence establishing the rape of Ms. Basu and the inability to link Mr. Sinha to any of the accusations, the court finds Mr. Sinha not guilty. The court orders that all charges against Mr. Sinha be dropped. Mr. Sinha, you are free to leave. The court is adjourned." The judge struck his gavel against the sound block and left the courtroom.

Kajal held Isa's hand. "I am sorry Isa. We tried our best."

Isa buried her face in her palms and wept.

Kajal looked at Leo. She then gathered her things and left the courtroom.

Leo walked up to Isa and sat next to her. "I'm really sorry, Isa. Let's go home."

Sinha shook hands with his lawyer. "I knew you were the man for the job."

Sinha's lawyer gloated. "Thank you, Mr. Sinha. Our justice system works. The innocent shouldn't have to pay a price for crimes they didn't commit." He winked at Sinha.

Sinha winked back at his lawyer. "I have you on speed dial. I will give you a lot of references."

Sinha's lawyer met Kajal in the hallway outside. "I was impressed at your composure today. You did a terrific job and reminded me of myself when I was a lot younger. You can have a tremendous future with my law firm should you choose to." He handed Kajal his business card.

Kajal took the card and ripped it to bits. "I will end myself before I sell my soul." She stormed off.

Inside the courtroom, Sinha celebrated with his wife. "Wait outside for me," he told his wife.

Sinha's wife quietly walked out of the courtroom.

Sinha walked over to where Isa and Leo sat. "You should've taken the money."

Isa froze.

Leo stood up. "The pain I am going to bring on you is going to make the sentence you would've gotten today seem like a walk in the park." Leo's eyes blazed. "You have two daughters, and one of them is a teenager."

Sinha cringed when Leo told him the name of the school his daughters went to.

Leo went closer to Sinha. "I will pay them a visit."

Sinha cowered.

Isa had gained composure. "We will make you pay for what you did, you bastard. You won't prey on anyone again."

Sinha hurried out of the courtroom.

The drive back to their apartments was quiet. Isa went into her apartment and locked the door. She curled up on her bed and cried.

Leo cracked open a beer. Sinha was the first criminal on his list and would be his initiation into his new world. Justice may have turned a blind eye on Isa, but Leo would unleash his wrath on Sinha. This was the beginning of the end for Sinha.

CHAPTER FIVE

CROSSING PATHS

Mumbai, March 2017

Sebastian's train that took him to his new life pulled up to the Lokmanya Tilak Terminus station, one of the busiest train stations in Mumbai. The long train ride seemed short to Sebastian, because he was excited and looked forward to this next chapter of his life. Sebastian got out of the train and looked around. He saw an ocean of people and wondered how anyone managed to move amid the chaos. He managed to spot the exit door and fought his way to it. Everyone was in a rush and people yelled into their cell phones nonstop.

Sebastian walked out of the door and found a less crowded spot. He took out his cell phone and called his new boss, who was picking him up at the station. Sebastian was bombarded by cab drivers who tried to convince him that their cab was the best and he would get the best deal with them. The phone he called rang and was answered by a man who talked loud and fast.

"This is Euro Bhai," the man on the other end of the phone yelled. Sebastian had to move the phone away from his ears. Bhai, which meant brother, was a term of respect, because he owned a company, and Euro was his company that worked mostly on European cars. "Where are you?" asked Euro Bhai animatedly.

"I am right outside the station standing under the large board with the name of the station on it." Sebastian looked around to see if he could spot Euro Bhai.

"What clothes are you wearing?" Euro Bhai yelled.

"Jeans and a black shirt," said Sebastian looking down at his clothes.

Euro Bhai chuckled. "Not very helpful. You are like half the other guys here. Lift both your arms all the way up and keep your index and little fingers on both hands pointed to the sky. Also lift your left leg off the ground."

"I am doing it," said Sebastian holding his phone to his ear using his shoulder. He felt a tap on his shoulder and turned around to see a tall and overweight man with a large moustache who grinned from ear to ear.

The large man put his cigarette butt on the ground and stomped it out. "Welcome to Mumbai. I am Munna, but everyone calls me Euro Bhai. I will be showing everyone at the garage this picture of you standing on one leg with your arms outstretched. You look like you are at a rock concert," said the man as he showed Sebastian the image on his phone. "The guys will get a kick out of it. In case you haven't realized, Sebastian, I was messing with you when I asked you to strike a pose. I knew exactly who you were because your old employer shared your picture with me."

Sebastian laughed sheepishly. "Thanks for picking me up."

"Are you hungry?" Euro Bhai took Sebastian's suitcase.

"I need to take a shower," said Sebastian." It's been a long train ride."

Euro Bhai put Sebastian's suitcase in the trunk. "The office is about eight miles from here, and the car ride will probably take about two hours."

Sabastian said "What?"

Euro Bhai looked amused. "This is Mumbai. Traffic is terrible. My first piece of advice is that you assume everyone in Mumbai is out to take advantage of you. Be very cautious while dealing with people."

Sebastian said he would keep that in mind.

Euro Bhai started the car. "My second piece of advice is that you never show fear. People here can smell fear, and they will target you if they sense fear. That's enough advice for today." Euro laughed and lit a cigarette. "Do you mind if I smoke?" Before Sebastian could answer, Euro Bhai interjected, "That's a rhetorical question. As you get to know me, you will realize that cigarettes are a big part of my life."

Sebastian smiled. "I don't have a problem with smoking. I used to be a smoker myself."

Euro put his car in gear and hit the gas. "What made you stop?"

"Life in general and they were an expensive habit," said Sebastian.

"Nobody is perfect." Euro Bhai took a long puff and honked on his horn multiple times as a man pushing a cart tried to cross the road in front of him.

"I really appreciate you giving me this opportunity, and I look forward to working with you," said Sebastian.

"Working for me," corrected Euro Bhai. "You have a long way to go before working with me."

"Understood," said Sebastian.

"Have you ever worked on European cars before?" Euro swerved, barely missing a cow that stood in the middle of the road.

"Mostly Indian and Japanese," said Sebastian.

"I expect you to watch and learn for the first few months, and then you can get your hands dirty. You will get a chance to work with Audis, VWs, BMWs, and maybe even some Porsches." He winked.

An hour and a half later Euro turned into a gate and pulled up to a two-story building. "We're here." A large billboard with the logos of European car companies stood in front of the building. It had the words Euro Motors painted on it. "Follow me." He introduced Sebastian to the four employees who worked for Euro Motors. He then took Sebastian behind the building. "This will be your new home." He pointed to a little room that stood beside the office building. "It's a small room, but people pay a lot of money for even smaller rooms in this location. There have been a few break-ins in the area, so you will also have the additional job of being the security guard. There is a small fridge in the office that you can use, and there is a stove if you decide you want to make food," said Euro Bhai. "Just don't burn the place down when you cook." He handed Sebastian a set of keys to the building and the little room.

"I don't know how to thank you," said Sebastian.

A few months had passed since Sebastian joined Euro Motors. He learned a lot about the business and the intricacies of working on European cars. Euro Bhai was impressed with the progress Sebastian had made and considered Sebastian his protégé. Sebastian enjoyed every minute of the work.

Euro Bhai came up to Sebastian one morning. "You have completed your probationary period, and you are ready to take on projects of your own. You will get a good raise and you will have additional responsibilities."

"Thanks, Bhai. That will really help my family." Sebastian had kept his expenses to a minimum and sent small amounts of money home that went toward family's debts. Life had given him a second chance, and he managed to turn things around.

One morning, Sebastian woke up early and got dressed in his overalls. He walked into the office and sat down at his desk, when his phone rang. "Come over to my office," said Euro Bhai and hung up.

Sebastian jumped out of his chair and walked up the flight of stairs that led to Euro Bhai's office. Euro Bhai's office was luxurious and gaudy. The man loved to project an image of luxury. Only high-paying customers got to see his office. Today was the first time Sebastian had gotten the opportunity to see it.

"Have a seat, Sebastian" said Euro Bhai, pointing to a plush blue leather chair. "We have a unique request from a customer, and I want to get your thoughts on it. The customer is a sixty-five-year-old doctor who owns a two thousand five Porsche 911 convertible with manual transmission. He bought the car in England brand new and had it shipped over when he moved back here. His car is his most prized possession, and it's in impeccable condition. He loves driving it and doesn't let anyone else drive the car. He has been diagnosed with rheumatoid arthritis and has shooting pains in his legs. He wants to know if we can modify his car so that he doesn't have to use his legs as much to drive. Are you able to do something like that?"

"How much time do I have to think about this?" Sebastian tried to contain his excitement. This was exactly the type of projects he wanted to get involved in.

"Take two days and come up with options and costs. We will talk through them before getting back to the doctor." Euro Bhai went back to typing on his computer.

"I'll get right on it." Sebastian jumped out of his chair.

"Good. Keep in mind that this will be our first modification job on a Porsche, and it will help our brand tremendously," said Euro Bhai.

Sebastian headed back to his desk with a spring in his step. His mechanical engineering major, although incomplete, had taught him invaluable lessons about design. The knowledge he had gained would help tremendously in this new project.

Sebastian reviewed his ideas with Euro Bhai and they decided to present it to the doctor. Euro Bhai called the doctor and scheduled an appointment.

The doctor brought his car in to Euro Motors. He met with Euro Bhai and Sebastian to discuss his options. "Welcome, doctor," said Euro Bhai. "Please have a seat."

The doctor sat down. "Let's get down to business, Euro Bhai."

Euro introduced Sebastian to the doctor. Sebastian took a marker and drew out the options on a white board to help the doctor visualize them. The doctor was satisfied.

The doctor stood up to leave. "Keep me posted about progress every week and treat her with respect." The doctor left Euro Bhai's office.

Sebastian spent most of his time working on the doctor's car. He called the doctor weekly and kept him updated on the progress. These days were the happiest of Sebastian's life because he was doing something he loved, something he was meant to do.

One afternoon Sebastian ate lunch at a small shack on the side of a one-lane highway very close to where he worked. Out of the corner of his eye he spotted a little boy with outstretched arms walking toward the highway. A bus sped down the highway.

"Stop!" yelled Sebastian. "Stop! There is a bus. You will get hit."

The boy didn't respond and kept walking. The boy was almost on the highway. Sebastian dashed out of the shack and ran toward the boy. The boy was on the highway and bus driver was too close to stop. Sebastian lunged forward and pulled the boy off the highway. The bus whizzed by with screeching tires. It passed inches away from Sebastian and the boy. Sebastian and the boy stumbled onto the ground. "What the hell were you thinking?" Sebastian screamed at the boy.

The boy howled and kept yelling for his mother. He still had his arms outstretched and was trying to feel his way around.

Sebastian realized that the little boy was blind.

A woman ran to the boy crying hysterically. She knelt and held the boy tight. The little boy stopped crying. "Thank you for saving my Anthony." The woman hugged Sebastian.

"It's no problem," said Sebastian, feeling uncomfortable at the public display of affection.

"He's everything I have, and I am everything he has." She had stopped crying. "My name is Anna."

"I didn't realize initially that he can't see," said Sebastian. "I was trying to get his attention from the shack, but he didn't hear or see me."

Anna put her hand lovingly on Anthony's head. "My Anthony is blind and deaf."

Sebastian looked at Anthony. "I'm so sorry. How old is he?"

"He's eight," said Anna. "As a token of gratitude for saving my son's life, I would like to invite you to our house for lunch one day."

"I would like that," said Sebastian.

Anna gave Sebastian her address.

Sebastian knelt in front of the boy and placed both his hands on the boy's shoulders. "I know that you can't hear me Anthony, but I am sorry for yelling at you."

Anna took Anthony's hand in hers. "I will see you soon. Thank you again for what you did for my son." Anna walked away holding Anthony's hand.

A few days later, Sebastian went to the address that Anna had given him. Her house was located on the second floor of a dilapidated building. He walked up a flight of stairs and knocked on the door.

Anna opened the door. "Welcome. Please come in. It's not much."

Anna's husband had died in an accident, and she lived in her mother-in-law's house. The house had one room that was divided into three sections using bed sheets. One section was where Anna's mother-in-law slept, the other was where Anna and Anthony slept, and the third was the kitchen. There was one shared bathroom in the building.

"Was Anthony born blind and deaf?" asked Sebastian as he ate rice and Bombay duck curry, a specialty fish curry of Mumbai. "I can't believe how cruel life is sometimes."

"He wasn't born like that. He has severe corneal damage, which has impacted his vision. He has a condition in his ear that caused hardening of the bones, leading to hearing loss." Anna sighed.

"Is there anything that can be done? A cure?" asked Sebastian.

"Both can be fixed by surgeries. Very expensive surgeries. Surgeries I cannot afford on my nurse's salary." Anna fought back tears, but a few found their way out.

"I'm sorry Anna. If I had the money, I would give it to you without thinking twice. I don't think there is a better use for money other than giving sight and hearing to a child." Sebastian enjoyed the simple yet delicious lunch.

"You are very kind." Anna put her hand on Sebastian's arm. Sebastian felt drawn to Anna. She was young, and life had been unfair to her.

It had taken her husband away and had given darkness to her child.

Sebastian and Anna became close. They called each other regularly and she visited Sebastian's little apartment at least once a week.

***

Sebastian had wrapped up work on the doctor's Porsche. He went to Euro Bhai's office and opened the door. "The car is ready for a test drive." He held up the keys to the doctor's Porsche.

"Great news. Right on schedule." Euro Bhai jumped out of his chair eagerly.

Sebastian had created a dual system in the car. The doctor could either drive the car as is or switch to the new system that Sebastian had put in place. Euro started the car and drove in normal mode. "The car drives exceptionally. The doctor sure takes good care of it." Euro drove down the highway and hit the gas. The car glided effortlessly.

"You ready to try the new system?" Sebastian asked enthusiastically.

Euro Bhai smiled. "You tell me when."

Sebastian instructed Euro Bhai to stop the car and turn it off. He pointed to a lever under the steering and asked Euro to shift it to the right position. "You are in the new mode now. Start the car."

"Thought there was going to be a loud noise or something." Euro Bhai joked. He started the car and put it in gear.

"I have added a display light to show what mode the car is in. In normal mode, the color is green, and in the new mode, it is red." Sebastian pointed to a small light on the dashboard that had turned red.

Euro Bhai's eyes opened wide.

Sebastian had built in a handle bar like that of a motorcycle. The doctor could change gears with his left hand and accelerate and brake with his right hand. The new mode took away use from the pedals and the steering wheel and diverted it through the new handlebar. The doctor could drive like normal when he didn't have shooting pains in his legs, and he could switch to the new mode when he did.

Euro grinned. "This is incredible. The car still drives exceptionally in the new mode. I'm amazed at how seamlessly the new mode engages, and how easy it is to drive." He drove the car back to his office.

Euro waved his hand. "Come to my office."

Sebastian followed him to his office, and Euro Bhai closed the door. "Today is a special occasion, and I have saved this for a day like today." He opened a wooden box and pulled out a bottle labeled Johnny Walker Blue Label aged twenty years. "The king of whiskeys."

Sebastian grabbed a couple of glasses and ice from the fridge.

Euro Bhai poured two large drinks and dropped cubes of ice in them. "A toast to you, Sebastian, the innovator, who is going to take Euro Motors to the next level." Euro Bhai raised his glass.

"Thank you. Does this mean I get to work with you and not for you?" Sebastian took a swig. The whiskey burned its way down.

"Indeed," said Euro Bhai. He was amused at the expression on Sebastian's face from the burn of the whiskey. "Sebastian, you are going to be the Porsche person. Any Porsche that comes into the garage will be your responsibility. I am going to call the doctor and tell him the great news. I will let him know that you will be taking his car to him. You can explain to him how everything works and let him test drive with you, so he feels comfortable." Euro finished his drink.

Sebastian thanked Euro Bhai and left his office. He finished up a few things and got in the doctor's car. It took three and a half hours of going through Mumbai traffic, getting around an accident, and taking multiple detours, before Sebastian reached the doctor's apartment building. The sky had gotten dark when he pulled up in front of the gate. The watchman recognized the car and opened the gate for him.

"The doctor is expecting you. You can park over to the right and then take the elevator to the eighth floor." Sebastian thanked him and drove to the parking spot.

The doctor's apartment was opened by a young man. "Please come in. My mother works for the doctor. The doctor takes a lot of medication and fell asleep about an hour ago. He was very excited to see his car but didn't manage to stay awake. The doctor asked if you could come tomorrow morning and show him how everything worked. He also asked me to give you dinner that he ordered from a really good restaurant nearby." The man took the keys from Sebastian.

Sebastian ate the meal with gusto. "Delicious. I didn't expect to be here this late. I was starving. Please thank the doctor for me." Sebastian got up and washed his hands. "Please tell the doctor that I will be here tomorrow morning." Sebastian felt sluggish after the heavy meal.

The young man handed Sebastian an envelope. "The doctor asked me to give this to you."

Sebastian opened the envelope once he was outside the apartment. There was a thank you note, and a wad of cash.

"Where can I get a cab?" Sebastian asked the watchman. The watchman told him that he could take a shortcut through a small alley that would connect to the main road where he would find a cab. Sebastian called Euro Bhai and told him that he had dropped off the car and would be heading to the doctor's house again in the morning.

He turned into the alley and started walking toward the main road ahead. The alley was deserted, and there were no street lights. A sudden movement to his right interrupted his thoughts. Before he could react, he felt a sharp pain on his shoulder. He collapsed to the ground clutching his shoulder and wincing in pain. When he looked up, he saw two men with their faces covered with masks standing over him.

"What the hell do you want?" Sebastian screamed.

"Money. We need money" said the man who had hit him with an iron rod.

"How much money do you have?" The second man holding a knife asked.

"I have about two hundred rupees." Sebastian stood up and reached into his pocket. He pulled out two bills. "Take it." He put the bills on the road.

The man holding the rod snatched the bills. "This is not enough to get us high."

The man holding the knife advanced. "Empty your pockets."

Sebastian took out his phone, and the man with the rod snatched it.

"Empty out your other pocket." The man with the knife was getting impatient.

"Fuck you," said Sebastian. "I gave you everything I have." He didn't want to give away the money the doctor had given him.

The man with the rod swung it at Sebastian's head. Sebastian blocked the blow with his arm. Sebastian lunged at the man with the rod. As he brawled, Sebastian felt a sharp pain on his left side below his ribs. He faltered and fell to the ground.

"What the fuck did you do?" The man with the rod screamed at the man with the knife. "All we were trying to do was get money for drugs, not kill someone. Let's get the fuck out of here," he yelled. The two men ran into the darkness.

Sebastian put pressure on the stab wound and stumbled toward the main road. He reached the main road and waved to cars passing by. None of the cars stopped, and he fell to his knees, weak from the blood loss.

***

Leo had convinced Isa to go out with him and try a new restaurant. She hadn't gone out anywhere besides college after the fateful day in court when she was denied justice. "This restaurant is in a five-star hotel, and the chef is a client of mine. He got me passes to the opening night today."

Leo and Isa got in his car and Leo drove to the restaurant. "Looking forward to trying something other than my terrible cooking?" Isa smiled weakly.

Leo chuckled. "Your cooking is excellent Isa." It was good to see Isa smile. "Smiling looks good on you." Leo pulled into the hotel parking lot and found an open spot. He came around and opened the door for Isa.

"Chivalry isn't dead after all." Isa stepped out of the car.

Leo closed the door. Leo and Isa went into the restaurant and got a table.

A voice behind Leo made him jump. "How are you son?" Anger filled Leo. "I am staying at this hotel for a few days. I saw you through the window as I was going out of the lobby."

Leo stood up and looked menacing. "Your son died the day he found out you were responsible for his mother's death."

A young woman came and stood beside his father. "How are you doing?" she asked.

Leo lost his temper. "Is this one of the prostitutes from your videos?" asked Leo, trying to keep calm.

"I am his wife," the young woman shrieked.

"Son, what happened to your mother-"

Leo cut him off before he could finish his sentence. "Don't ever utter my mother's name. It should have been you who died, not my mother." Leo turned to Isa. "I'm sorry you had to witness this Isa. Let's go somewhere else."

Isa stood up looking shocked. Leo took Isa's arm and walked to his car.

"Why are you so upset with your father, Leo? You never told me about him. I'm not used to seeing you this way." Isa put an arm on Leo's shoulder.

"He is not worth mentioning. He is not in my life." Leo tightened his grip on the steering wheel. He sped out of the parking lot.

Isa looked out of the car and squinted. "There is a man lying on the side of the road," Isa yelled.

Leo turned the car around and pulled up next to Sebastian. He jumped out of the car and knelt beside Sebastian. "What happened? Are you okay?"

"I was stabbed," whimpered Sebastian. "I feel dizzy."

"You have lost a lot of blood," said Isa. "We need to get you to a hospital."

Leo carried Sebastian to the car and laid him down on the back seat.

Isa put pressure on Sebastian's wound, so he wouldn't bleed out.

"Hang in there, buddy. I am going to drive us to the nearest hospital," said Leo. He put the car in gear and floored it.

A short drive later, Leo pulled into a hospital and stopped the car right outside the front door. "I have an emergency," he yelled. "This man has been stabbed and has lost a lot of blood."

Hospital attendants brought a gurney and wheeled Sebastian in.

"We should wait for a while," said Isa.

Leo and Isa went to the waiting room. Sebastian was wheeled into the intensive care unit with doctors and nurses going in with him.

One of the doctors eventually came out of the room and told Leo and Isa. "He is stable, but he's lost a lot of blood and needs a blood transfusion as soon as possible. His blood type is AB negative, a rare type. We don't have AB negative blood in the hospital blood bank. We are trying to reach other blood banks to see if we can source blood, but you need to try to find a donor, so we can get the transfusion started as soon as possible. Time is of the essence," said the doctor and walked away.

"No shit, Sherlock," muttered Leo.

"Know anyone with AB negative blood?" asked Isa.

"I don't know if I do or not," said Leo. "Haven't really asked anyone what their blood type is."

"Eureka," said a voice behind Leo and Isa. They turned around to see a chubby man with thick glasses and a baby face.

"I'm sorry?" asked Leo.

"Eureka," said the chubby man.

Leo threw his hands up in the air. "What do you want?"

The man took off his glasses and wiped them on his shirt. "It's what Archimedes, the Greek mathematician and inventor shouted while running through the streets of Greece after discovering the principle of displacement," the chubby man said.

"I think you have the wrong hospital," said Leo. "This isn't a psychiatric hospital."

The baby-faced man chuckled. "Most geniuses have a bit of lunacy living within them," said the man.

"Okay, baby-faced genius, we are in the middle of something urgent and can't waste time," Leo said.

"My handsome friend," the baby-faced man said. "Eureka is an expression to celebrate finding something."

"What the hell have we found?" asked Leo, losing his patience.

"You have found me," said the man. "I wasn't eavesdropping, but I overheard your conversation about needing AB negative blood. My blood is AB negative. So Eureka." He winked.

Isa went over and put her arm through his. "Not only is he a genius, but he is also rare," said Isa. "What is thy name, oh wise one?"

"Friends call me Walt," the man said. "Got the name in college when I was studying chemistry, and it stuck. I had the ability to mix chemicals to get my friends high, and they gave me the name. It is from the series, *Breaking Bad*."

Leo raised his eyebrows. "Are you a drug dealer?"

"I am a chemist. I came to the hospital for work," said Walt. "Let's go donate my blood."

Leo knocked on the doctor's door. "Eureka," said Leo. He winked at Isa and Walt.

"What?" asked the doctor.

"We found our AB negative donor, Doc." Leo pointed at Walt.

Walt took a bow that caused Isa to chuckle.

"Incredible news," said the doctor. "Follow me. Let's get the process started."

"If you'll excuse me," said Walt. "I got a life to save."

Leo chuckled.

Isa rolled her eyes.

Leo and Isa headed to the waiting room and sat down. "Hell of a night," said Isa.

The doctor later came to Leo and Isa. "Everything went smoothly, and Walt should be out in an hour or so. Sebastian will make a full recovery. You guys saved his life. If you hadn't found him when you did, he could've died."

"You saved his life, Doc." Leo shook the doctor's hand.

"Sebastian doesn't have medical insurance, and he will be responsible to pay out of pocket," the doctor said.

Walt came to the waiting room shortly. "Saving lives makes me hungry and thirsty. I need food and beer."

"Food and beer on me, superhero, said Leo. "Let's head to my apartment."

CHAPTER SIX

BONDING THROUGH DARKNESS

Mumbai, June 2017

Isa, Walt, and Leo visited Sebastian in the hospital the next morning. The nurse on duty took them into Sebastian's room, where he lay awake but still in a lot of pain.

Sebastian managed to smile weakly when he saw the three of them walk in. "Thanks for saving my life." Sebastian tried to sit up and winced in pain.

"Save your energy," said Leo. "The nurse told us that you will be here for a few more days."

"I don't know how to thank all of you," said Sebastian. "The nurse told me that you guys paid all my bills. I would like to know how much I owe you. It will take me some time, but I will pay it back."

"We'll worry about that later," said Leo. "Here is my phone number. If you need anything, just text or call." Leo left a piece of paper on the table next to Sebastian's bed.

"The two guys who did this to me took my phone. A policeman came earlier this morning and took my statement," said Sebastian. "I called my boss this morning from the hospital phone and let him know what is going on. He said he would stop by later." Sebastian picked up the piece of paper. "I need to get a new phone."

"Hope the police get the guys who did this to you. You focus on getting better, Sebastian," said Isa. "We will catch up when we can." Isa left a basket of fruit on the table for Sebastian. They bid him goodbye and left the hospital.

A few days later, Leo received a text message from Sebastian letting him know that he was out of the hospital and back to work.

Leo invited Isa, Sebastian, and Walt for dinner and drinks at his apartment. Sebastian was the first to arrive at Leo's place. He rang Leo's doorbell.

"Come on in Sebastian." Leo held the door open and ushered him in. "Good to see you standing up."

Sebastian came bearing gifts in the form of bottles of alcohol.

"You have good taste in booze, my friend," said Leo. "This is going to be the beginning of a long friendship."

Sebastian chuckled. He put the bottles on the kitchen counter. "I feel so much better. Thankfully, it was a small knife. I am back at work but can't do any heavy lifting yet. It's thanks to you guys that I am alive." Sebastian took a seat on the couch.

The doorbell rang twice. Leo opened the door and saw Walt standing outside with a big grin and a case of beer.

"I see that your diet is going very well," said Leo, punching Walt's belly.

"For sure, my brother," said Walt. "You have a six pack, and I have two twelve packs," said Walt, lifting his case of beer.

Leo laughed at his comment.

There was a knock on the door, and Leo opened it to see Isa standing outside. "Isa, you look beautiful, as always." Leo held the door open for her.

Isa blushed. "For a man who knows so many women, you look like you are seeing a woman for the first time," she said, catching Leo's stare.

"What do you mean so many women?" Leo asked.

"I am your neighbor. I can see and hear all the women coming in and out of here," said Isa. She walked into the apartment as Leo smiled sheepishly.

"You look all healed up." Isa walked over to Sebastian and hugged him.

Sebastian's face flushed. "Thanks to you guys, I am alive." Said Sebastian.

"We were at the right place at the right time," said Isa, sitting next to Sebastian.

"Did you start to feel powerful once you received my blood?" Walt asked, and Sebastian chuckled. Isa rolled her eyes and Leo punched Walt playfully in the gut.

The night of drinking that ensued created a bond among the four acquaintances. The alcohol took away all inhibitions, and the inebriated friends confided in each other.

Walt was the first to share his story about how he ended up in Mumbai. "My real name is Raghu Iyer. My father, a renowned astrologer, was nicknamed Nostradam-Iyer after the French astrologer Nostradamus, by some of his clients, who claimed he had accurately predicted events in their lives. His arrogance knew no bounds." He slurred from all the shots of whiskey. "My little sister, who meant the world to me, died in a car crash. I called my father a fraud because he couldn't predict the untimely death of his own daughter. After my sister's death, I couldn't see eye to eye with my father and I started using drugs. My mother saw that I was heading down a destructive path. She sold her family heirloom jewelry she was saving for my sister's wedding and contacted her cousin in Mumbai asking him to help me get my life back on track. My mother's cousin got me admitted to a bachelor's degree in Chemistry at the university where he worked. I completed my degree and now work for a big pharmaceutical company as a chemist and spend most of my time in a lab. My mother is my rock, and I talk to her a few times a week. I haven't spoken to my father since I left home." Walt had tears in his eyes. "If I wasn't invited here today, I would probably be in my lab doing research and then at home drinking myself to sleep." Walt took a shot of whiskey followed by a large swig of beer.

"Sorry to hear about your sister," said Isa. She took Walt's hand in hers and squeezed it gently.

"Thanks Isa. This is the first time I have spoken to anyone about the darkness that haunts me. Now you guys can't get rid of me even if you want to. You will be stuck being my friends." Walt got fist bumps from Leo and Sebastian.

"We'll keep you around. You never know when we might need AB negative blood," said Leo with a chuckle.

"To AB negative blood donors." Walt raised his glass of Whiskey. He gulped it down and lay on the floor. A few moments later Walt was snoring.

"To lightweight AB negative blood donors." Leo raised his glass as Sebastian and Isa burst out laughing.

"What about you, Sebastian?" asked Isa. "How did you end up in Mumbai?" Isa sipped on her first glass of wine of the evening.

Sebastian was usually a man of few words, but six drinks made him loquacious. "My life was touched by darkness just like Walt's. I came to the city of dreams to escape that darkness. I grew up in Bangalore in a lower-middle-class family. I was interested in cars growing up and worked part-time at the neighborhood car repair shop since I was fifteen. By the time I was eighteen, I could fix most problems with cars, and I could take apart and put most car parts together." Sebastian paused to take a sip of his drink. "I was in my happy place when I worked on cars. When I turned eighteen, I got admitted into the mechanical engineering program in the Indian Institute of Engineering, Bangalore, one of the most prestigious engineering colleges in the country. It was a very expensive program and my father took out hefty loans to send me there. I met a professor in college who got me an internship in Germany with Porsche. I was to fly to Germany as soon as I graduated." Sebastian's eyes lit up when he talked about his college days.

"The Porsche?" asked Leo.

"Yeah," said Sebastian.

"Impressive, man," said Leo.

"Well, my life took a turn, a turn for the worse. I met a woman in college during my third year. She came into my life like a whirlwind and turned it upside down. Before I met her, I spent every hour I wasn't in class in the library doing research or working on assignments. She was charismatic and had a way of getting me to do things." Sebastian took a large sip of his drink. He slurred while he spoke again. "She was the first woman I'd been with. She even had me dress up like a woman and sneak into her dorm room."

"Men have done crazier things to make women happy," said Leo.

"I don't even want to know," said Isa. She rolled her eyes.

"We were dating, and we were serious about each other. I was very clear with her about going to Germany right after I finished my final semester exams. I told her that once I settled down and had a permanent job, we could take things to the next level. She had other plans. We were in our last semester and had one month to go before our final exams. She came up to me one day in the library and told me that she didn't want me to go to Germany. I lost my temper and told her that I was very clear with her about going. She walked away with tears in her eyes. Later I was sitting in my classroom working on assignments when she walked in. It was just the two of us in the room. She came up to me and ripped her clothes. She then ripped my shirt and scratched my face. She screamed for help and sank her nails into me. I tried to pull her off me, but I couldn't. I lost my temper and slapped her. A teacher who had run into the room hearing her scream witnessed me slapping her. The teacher told me to back off and took me to the dean's office. The woman I was dating accused me of trying to rape her. The teacher told the dean what she had witnessed. The woman I dated did a hell of a job portraying me as an animal. The dean expelled me. I didn't graduate and lost my internship with Porsche." Sebastian sighed and gulped down his drink.

Leo fixed him another.

"Isa, I have never laid a finger on a woman before or after. I am sorry, and I just wanted to clarify that." Sebastian lowered his gaze.

"I believe you, Sebastian. You didn't have a choice in that situation. I don't think you are the type of person to harm a woman. What happened then?"

The kindness and sincerity in Isa's voice made Sebastian feel better. "My parents were devastated but they told me that it wasn't my fault. I went back to work at my neighborhood car shop for a year or so. The owner of the car shop found out that an old friend of his was opening a car company in Mumbai that specialized in European cars. The owner called his friend and got me a job here. That is how I ended up in Mumbai. I am enjoying my work here and learning a lot about European cars. I was on my way back after delivering my first Porsche when I got stabbed. You guys know the rest." Sebastian put his head back on the couch.

"I am sorry about what happened to you in college. It's incredible that people can be so inconsiderate." Isa put her hand on Sebastian's shoulder. She then excused herself to use the restroom. When she got back, Sebastian was passed out on the couch. Leo stood on his balcony and sipped on a beer.

Isa came and stood by Leo. "I can't believe the stuff Walt and Sebastian have gone through."

"The reason all of us get along so well is because we have all been touched by darkness," Leo said.

"You need to tell me your story, Leo. I have never seen you react the way you did when you saw your father." Isa looked at Leo.

"This is the first time you are standing on my side of the balcony, Isa." Leo held her hand. "Are you sure you want to hear my story? It's not a happy one."

"I do," said Isa.

"My father, the man you saw the other day, destroyed my mother's and my life. He was someone I looked up to and respected until I was twenty-one years old. He named me after Leonardo da Vinci, the Italian artist and designer, who my father respected a lot."

"You look like a Leonardo. It's the perfect name for you." Isa looked lovingly into Leo's eyes.

"I was born in Cochin, Kerala, in a house on the banks of the backwaters. Have you been to Kerala?"

"No, I haven't," said Isa.

"I will take you there someday. My father was a well-known surgeon and traveled a lot. He was a connoisseur of art, and the house where I was born was a thing of beauty. My father had a lot of Leonardo da Vinci replicas. When I was three years old, my mother fell from the top of the house and died. I don't remember any of that, but that's what I was told until I was twenty-one. I was sent to Kodaikanal, to boarding school, when I was five. My school teachers were more like parents to me than my dad ever was. I used to come home once a year for a few weeks, but my dad was traveling most of the time. I finished my undergraduate degree in political science from Delhi and was admitted to a law program in Harvard. I spent a few months at home before heading to Boston to pursue my law degree. On my twenty-first birthday, my life was turned upside down. My father called me and told me he would be home in a couple of days to celebrate my birthday. It was later that day I received the letter that devastated my life. A letter addressed to me from my mother." Leo's hand shook.

Isa squeezed Leo's hand tight. "Is this going to be too hard for you?"

"I think this will be good for me, Isa. I haven't told anyone my story. It will be good to get it off my chest," said Leo. "The letter started by my mother telling me how much she loved me and how much she regretted the path she had chosen. The letter then told me that my mother had taken her own life." Leo choked, and his body trembled.

"I'm sorry." Isa held him tight.

"My mother stumbled upon something that led her to believe she didn't have another choice. Taking her life was her only way out. I was devastated when I read the letter. I remember wondering if my father could really be the sexual fiend that my mother described him to be. He wasn't a big part of raising me, but he had given me the best of everything. I wondered how my father could keep from me the fact that my mother took her own life. I sat in my room and cried awhile and then decided to go to my father's office referenced in my mother's letter. I stood outside his office and thought about the numerous times I had been in there. It was where my father used to teach me about da Vinci's works. He had numerous replicas of paintings and sculptures of da Vinci's works in his office. I hadn't been in his office in many years. When I opened the door, I smelled the familiar smell of cigars and whiskey. I looked around the office and walked towards the wooden "Vitruvian Man" statue mentioned in my mother's letter. I used to play around this statue as a kid. I snapped the head forward exactly as mentioned in my mother's letter. There was a red button underneath the head, as the letter explained. I pushed the red button. I heard a creak behind me, and a section of the wall opened. I pulled it wide open and entered the secret room and went to the cabinets. When I opened the cabinets, I saw the collection of VHS tapes just like my mother's letter had described. I turned on the television and loaded a tape that was dated a few days after my mothers' death. The images showed my father engaging in disturbing sexual acts. I was appalled by the number of tapes and the fact that there were tapes dated the day of my birth and a few days after my parents wedding. My mother had stumbled on this room, and it had pushed her over the edge. My innocent and pious mother couldn't accept the fact that her husband was an animal. My world was shaken by the revelation that my whole life was a lie. I took all the tapes outside and set fire to them." Leo had tears in his eyes.

"I can't believe you went through so much pain. Unless you had told me your story, I wouldn't have guessed that you had gone through something so dark. You are such a positive person." Isa teared up.

"I left my house the day I read my mother's letter. The first time I saw or talked to my father since I left home was when we saw him at the restaurant. My mother left me a good amount of money, and that was her way of ensuring that I would be financially independent. I picked Mumbai as my destination." Leo turned to face Isa.

"I'm glad you picked Mumbai. Otherwise we wouldn't have met," said Isa.

Leo leaned in to kiss Isa.

Every impulse in Isa's body told her to reciprocate. "I'm sorry, Leo. I'm not ready yet. I need some more time."

"I'm sorry," said Leo backing away.

"Don't be. I just need some time." Isa went back to her apartment.

Leo went to his bedroom and passed out on the bed. He woke up the next morning and went into his living room. Walt had left, and Sebastian was still asleep on the sofa. Sebastian woke up a while later to the smell of eggs and coffee.

"How's the hangover?" asked Leo.

Sebastian clutched his head. "I'm never drinking again."

"Until next weekend," said Leo with a chuckle. "I'm making omelets. They should help with the hangover."

Sebastian took a shower and came into the living room. He found a plate with a large omelet waiting for him. "That smells amazing," said Sebastian.

"Dig in," said Leo. "There is coffee and orange juice as well."

"Are you seeing anyone in Mumbai? Do you have a girlfriend?" asked Leo and took a sip of his orange juice.

"I think so," said Sebastian with an awkward smile.

Leo chuckled. "You either do or you don't."

Sebastian told Leo about how he had met Anna and Anthony. "She is an incredible woman. Life hasn't been fair to her." Sebastian took a sip of coffee. "Her little boy who is deaf and blind is only eight years old. I can't imagine someone so little going through so much." Sebastian stared at his plate.

"That's terrible. What happened to him?" Leo asked.

"Here's the thing. His hearing and sight defects can be corrected by surgery, very expensive surgery. Anna works as a nurse in a government hospital and can't afford to pay for the surgeries. I wish there was a way to get him the help that he needs. If I had the money, I would give it to him." Sebastian put his fork down on the table.

"How much do the surgeries cost?" Leo asked.

"Anna told me that it was going to be a little over a million rupees." Sebastian shook his head.

Leo had about seven million rupees left in the account his mother had left him. His mother would have given the money to save a child's life without hesitation. A plan formed in his head. "I can help Anthony," said Leo.

"What do you mean?" Sebastian put his fork and knife down.

"My mother left me money before she died, and I haven't had to use much of it. My job pays my bills, and I don't currently have plans for the money she left me." Leo finished his omelet.

"Leo, I can't take your money. You don't even know Anthony," said Sebastian.

"Listen to me carefully, Sebastian." Leo crossed his arms. "I will need something in return. Something that is dangerous and risky. We will not only give sight and hearing to Anthony, but also protect potential victims from a predator."

"I'm not...I'm not sure I understand. Dangerous? Predator?" Sebastian shifted nervously in his chair.

"There is a criminal who has raped multiple times and escaped through the cracks in our justice system," said Leo.

Sebastian looked confused.

Leo leaned forward in his chair. "I intend to take this man down hard and get him punished to the full extent of the law."

"How is that related to Anna and Anthony?" Sebastian asked.

"We could use Anthony to take this man down for good. The plan will be designed to ensure that no harm will come to Anthony. Talk it over with Anna and let me know." Leo stood up and took his plate to the sink.

"I will talk it over with Anna. If we can guarantee that no harm comes to Anthony, I think she will agree. Let me go talk to her right away. I will call you later." Sebastian washed his dishes and left Leo's apartment. He headed straight to Anna's house.

CHAPTER SEVEN

DAY OF RECKONING

Mumbai, August 2017

Leo's phone rang. He walked to a quieter area of the gym and picked it up. "Hey, Leo, it's Sebastian," said the voice on the other line. "I spoke to Anna. Can you meet for a bit? Anna wants to talk to you."

"Hold on for a minute." Leo checked his schedule on his phone. "Can you meet in two hours? I will be done with my next client in an hour and a half."

"Absolutely. I will pick up Anna and head toward your gym. We will get there in two hours," said Sebastian.

"Perfect. There is a coffee shop close to my gym. I will text you the name and address. There are tables outside, and we can talk discreetly. See you guys soon." Leo hung up and pulled up the address of the coffee shop. He texted the address to Sebastian and received a thumbs-up emoji.

Leo arrived at the coffee shop a few minutes early and went to the counter. "Three cardamom chais please." Leo paid and waited. Once he got the chais, he headed outside to find a table. He took a seat at a table that was the farthest away from other tables. This setup ensured complete privacy during his conversation with Sebastian and Anna. He took a sip of his chai and smacked his lips. The intense aroma and sweet flavor of cardamom reminded of him of home.

Sebastian walked into the coffee shop with Anna and took a seat at the table. "Leo, this is Anna."

Leo stood up.

Anna pressed her hands together in front of her chest. "Namaste." Her palms touched, and her fingers pointed upwards.

"Namaste, Anna. Please have a seat." Leo pointed to the chair. He bumped fists with Sebastian. "Please have some tea."

Sebastian and Anna sipped on their tea.

"I am really sorry to hear about your son's condition," said Leo. He took a large sip of his tea.

"He is a strong boy," said Anna. "If not for Sebastian, he wouldn't be in this world anymore and neither would I."

Sebastian turned red.

Leo patted Sebastian on the back. "Sebastian told me how strong Anthony is. Look Anna, I would like to help your son, but I will need something from him and you in exchange." Leo leaned forward in his chair.

"What? What do you want from us? I will do anything for him to get the surgeries he needs but I won't do anything that puts my son in danger." Anna trembled.

"I would never put your son in any kind of danger. What I am proposing is for him to be part of a plan that will help us take down a dangerous criminal and rapist. This animal has raped multiple times and gotten away with it. I promise that your son will be in our sight the whole time. You will be there with us when we execute the plan. If you feel unsafe in the slightest, you can pull the plug on the plan and I will still give you the money for your son's surgery."

Anna looked at Sebastian nervously. Sebastian told Anna that it was going to be okay.

Leo walked Sebastian and Anna through his plan. The time and place were yet to be finalized, but he had crafted a twisted plan to take Sinha down. Anna was hesitant at first, but once she was convinced that her son wouldn't be in danger, she agreed. Two other things led her to agree. One was that her son was going to play a big part in taking down a criminal. The second was that since he couldn't see or hear anything, he wouldn't need to know what was happening. She was desperate for Anthony to get his sight and hearing back. "I want to be there when everything goes down. Thank you for helping my son." She stood up and folded her arms. She started to walk out.

"I will call you later," Sebastian called out to Leo as he followed Anna to the door.

Leo finished his tea and headed back to the gym. He was one step closer to taking down Sinha and getting justice for Isa.

Leo took a couple of days off from work and started his reconnaissance. He woke up early and drove to Sinha's house. He parked in his car across the street from Sinha's house and waited. The ornate gate of Sinha's house opened, and a black Mercedes SUV with lightly tinted windows drove out. Sinha sat in the back seat while two large men sat in the front. Leo took out his phone and made an entry of the date and time Sinha left the house. He then followed the SUV. It reached Sinha's office building and pulled into the parking lot. Leo stayed around the office building for the next few hours.

Sinha's car came out of the office parking lot around noon. Leo made another entry on his phone. He followed the SUV to a country club thirty minutes away. It was an exclusive golf club and resort that only members who paid exorbitant fees had access to. The restaurant and bar attached to the club were open to anyone who wanted to wine and dine there. Leo pulled into the guest parking lot and went into the bar. He ordered a drink while watching Sinha play poker inside a room with glass walls. It was a sit-and-go session and went on for an hour. Post poker, lunch was served, which was finished in thirty minutes. Sinha's bodyguards sat in the restaurant stuffing their faces from the buffet.

After lunch Sinha met his bodyguards at the lobby. One of the bodyguards went to get Sinha's car. Sinha left the club two hours after he had arrived. Leo followed Sinha's SUV. Sinha's next stop was his office, where he spent two hours before heading back to the country club. Leo documented Sinha's schedule and went home.

The next morning, he followed Sinha to the office and then to the country club. This time, instead of sitting at the bar, Leo went to the parking lot where Sinha's SUV was parked. He took out the magnetic GPS tracking device he had bought online and attached it to the undercarriage of Sinha's SUV. He checked to make sure he got a signal and then drove away from the country club.

Sinha was a creature of habit. Leo tracked Sinha and found that he followed the same schedule. Friday, around noon, Sinha's GPS showed a new route. The signal showed Sinha's SUV drive out of Mumbai. It came to stop after an hour and a half. Sinha's SUV stayed in the area for a few hours before it started moving. The signal showed the SUV make the hour-and-a-half drive into Mumbai and come to a stop at Sinha's house around nine at night.

Sinha followed the same schedule on Friday the following week. Leo was curious about Sinha's trip out of Mumbai, which made him decide to follow Sinha on the following Friday.

Leo drove to Sinha's office building a few minutes before noon and parked his car across the street. Sinha's SUV came out of the office gate at noon, just like clockwork. Leo followed the SUV as it drove out of Mumbai. Sinha's SUV pulled up to a house on a small and isolated beach. Sinha got out of his car carrying a briefcase. He gave instructions to his bodyguards, and they took off in the SUV.

Leo parked his car about two hundred feet away from the house and walked toward it. He circled the house and hid behind a palm tree when he saw Sinha. Sinha came out on the patio dressed in shorts and a T-shirt. He set a bottle of whiskey, club soda, and ice on a patio table. He sat on a recliner with a drink in his hand. He was oblivious to the fact that he was being watched from a few feet away. He took out his phone and got lost in it. He finished his drink and made himself another. As he sat on the recliner with his second drink, his phone rang. He picked up a second phone from the pocket of his shorts. "Is she young?" He cackled. "Great, she is a college student, and this is her first time. Can't wait to meet her." He laughed loudly. "I will make it worth her while. Call me when you are outside." Sinha hung up the phone and smacked his lips.

Leo was consumed by rage when he heard Sinha talk about exploiting a young woman. He felt the urge to end Sinha right there. He stopped himself, because he realized that death would be too easy. He wanted Sinha to suffer. He wanted Sinha to want death but not get it.

Sinha's phone rang again. "You are here with the girl? I am coming. Of course I have your payment. I am your best customer." Sinha gulped down his drink and jumped out of his chair. He headed into the house and closed the door behind him.

Leo felt disgusted as he walked back to his car. He needed to make sure that Sinha was completely cut off from society and couldn't continue his atrocities. Leo waited in his car. He saw a young woman come out of Sinha's house in tears. A man got out of a beaten-up car and grabbed the young woman. He forced her into the car and drove away. Sinha's SUV pulled in front of the beach house. Sinha got into the SUV looking smug.

Leo had decided on the location for his plan. Sinha's beach house was the perfect spot to take him down. Leo decided to do it two Fridays from that day. Isa was going out of town for two weeks to visit her grandparents. Leo didn't want Isa to be part of it, as neither Sebastian not Walt knew what Sinha had done to her. Sinha would rot in prison. It had to be done as soon as possible, because he couldn't let Sinha exploit more women.

There were two vital payers in Leo's plan. One was Anthony, the little boy, and the second was Suzanna, a college student from Spain whom Leo had met in Goa. It wasn't a complicated plan, and Leo was confident that Suzanna could entice Sinha. They needed to bring Anna up to speed.

Leo met with Walt and Sebastian and went over the plan. "What do you guys think?" asked Leo.

"One ought to be afraid of nothing other than things possessed of power to do us harm, but things innocuous need not be feared," said Walt.

Sebastian threw his arms in the air. "What the hell? Translate please."

"It's a quote from "Dante's Inferno", the divine comedy," said Walt tightening his jaw. "What I meant to say is, let's destroy him. I'm in."

Five days to go before Sinha would be taken down. Isa was flying to Kolkata to visit her grandparents in a few hours. Leo volunteered to drive Isa to the airport.

Isa answered her doorbell. "Thanks for dropping me off," she said.

Leo took the suitcase from Isa. "My pleasure. I hope you have a great time back home visiting your grandparents." Leo pushed the button to summon the elevator.

"I'm sure the first thing they will say is that I am too skinny and that I need to eat." Isa laughed. The elevator door opened, and Leo held it open for Isa. "Always the gentleman."

"Mumbai will miss you," said Leo. He pushed the button marked lobby and the doors closed.

"I will miss Mumbai too," said Isa. The silence in the elevator was broken by the beep as the elevator reached the lobby.

Leo dropped Isa at the airport and went back home. His friend Suzanna was flying into Mumbai the next day and would stay with him until Friday. Once they were finished with Sinha, she would fly back to Goa and then to Barcelona, Spain, two days later.

Leo drove to the airport the next evening to pick up Suzanna. He pulled over by the arrivals gate and looked around. There was a knock on the passenger window, and Suzanna appeared with a huge smile. Her hazel eyes were enchanting and her dimples accentuated the mischief in her eyes. Her silky brown hair bounced over her shoulder.

Suzanna put her duffel bag in the back seat and got into the passenger's seat. "Hey handsome." She leaned over and kissed Leo on the cheek.

Leo kissed her on the cheek. "How does it feel to be the most beautiful woman in Mumbai?"

Suzanna giggled. "I see that you haven't forgotten your pick-up lines."

Leo held her hand. "You sure about doing this?"

"I would've overdosed if you hadn't found me in Goa. This is the least I can do to repay you. Also, if this man is the predator you say he is, I am happy to stop him from hurting other women." She squeezed Leo's hand.

Leo had met Suzanna at a party in Goa a few months earlier. Suzanna was from Barcelona, Spain, and was backpacking through India. Leo had found her passed out at a party in a beach resort in Goa. Her lips were blue, and she wasn't responsive. He gave her rescue breathing and resuscitated her. She threw up a few times before she regained her senses. Someone in the group she was hanging out with had given her ecstasy pills. The last thing she remembered was popping one of them. Suzanna and Leo had spent passionate nights in Goa together before they parted ways.

Leo had called Suzanna a few weeks earlier asking if she could come over to Mumbai and help him out with the Sinha situation. She was going to be instrumental in taking down Sinha.

Suzanna ran her fingers through Leo's hair. "I missed you and your body. I thought a lot about you and the time we spent in Goa." Suzanna ran her hands over Leo's chest and arms.

Leo thought about the wild nights in Goa with Suzanna. He hit the gas harder, hoping to reach home faster, but had to hit the brakes hard because he almost slammed into another car. Who was he kidding? They were stuck in Mumbai traffic, and it would take them at least another hour.

The drive to his apartment building seemed endless, but they finally made it. Leo pulled his car into his parking spot. He circled around and opened the door for Suzanna. He grabbed her bag from the car, and they walked to the lobby. As soon as the elevator doors closed, Suzanna grabbed Leo and placed her lips on his. They kissed passionately and didn't notice that the elevator had come to a halt.

The door opened and an elderly couple stood outside. The woman's mouth dropped when she saw the public display of passion. The older man stared as Leo and Suzanna kissed. The woman cleared her throat loudly, causing Leo and Suzanna to pull apart. She stormed into the elevator looking livid. Leo and Suzanna walked out of the elevator, and Suzanna gave the older man a wink. While the doors were closing, the older man gave Leo and Suzanna a sweet toothless smile and a thumbs up. Suzanna blew a kiss to the old man, which made the woman more upset.

Suzanna grabbed Leo's arms and pulled him onto the balcony as soon as they were inside the apartment. Leo turned off the lights so that no one would see them on his balcony. They kissed while they removed each other's clothes. Leo turned Suzanna around. She groaned as Leo grabbed her hair and took her from behind. She moaned and squealed over the next few agonizingly pleasurable minutes and then dug her nails into Leo's thighs as she orgasmed with a scream.

She turned around and kissed Leo. "I craved you," she said.

Leo picked her up and carried her to the bedroom. He gently laid her on the bed and got on top of her. Suzanna rolled over, got up, pushed Leo onto the bed and got on top of him. She tied both his arms to the bedposts.

"I am the one in control usually, but this is a welcome surprise," said Leo as she tightened the knots.

Suzanna kissed Leo and slowly moved down his body.

Leo felt his muscles tense up.

She rode him at first with a slow, steady rhythm and then moaned loudly as she went faster. She set off a shattering moan and dug her fingers into Leo's chest as her eyes rolled into the back of her head. She collapsed on top of Leo and kissed him. She untied his arms and lay on the bed.

"My turn," said Leo, and tied her arms to the bedposts. He kissed her on the lips hungrily. He then moved slowly down her neck to her firm breasts and gave them his undivided attention. Suzanna went crazy and made raw and delicious sounds of pleasure as Leo played with her nipples with his tongue. As Leo went lower down her belly, her back arched and her mouth opened wide while her body quivered. Leo started thrusting gently and steadily at first. Her back arched higher and she shuddered as Leo's tempo increased. Leo grabbed her hair with one hand and her throat with the other. With her eyes rolled into the back of her head and her toes curled, she let out a

Bonded by Darkness

loud scream and almost lifted Leo off the bed with her arched back. Leo let out a primal grunt as he climaxed. He felt invincible as both collapsed onto the bed. Leo untied Suzanna's arms and they lay in bed until their hearts beat at their normal rhythm.

"I am yours, Leo. You know how to drive a woman crazy." Suzanna placed her head on Leo's chest.

The night before Sinha would be taken down arrived faster than expected. Leo made a call to Walt. "Is the tranquilizer ready?"

"Ready and packed. There are two vials. It will knock Sinha out for about ten minutes. I have tested it three times on myself and timed it." Walt chuckled.

Leo shook his head in disbelief. "You tested it on yourself? Are you crazy?"

"This is all-natural stuff. No harmful side effects and cannot be detected by toxicology tests." Walt sounded confident.

Leo was satisfied.

"Tomorrow is the day, my friend. I will see you bright and early." Leo hung up the phone.

His next call was to Sebastian, who answered the phone with a tremor in his voice. "Are Anna and Anthony ready?" Leo asked.

"They are ready. We haven't done anything like this before. We're all nervous."

"Everything will be okay. I will see you at Sinha's beach house tomorrow."

108

Suzanna and Leo picked up Walt and drove to Sinha's beach house the next day. Leo parked away from Sinha's beach house and waited.

Sebastian's loaner car from his workshop pulled up right behind Leo's car. Through his rearview mirror, Leo saw that Anna and Anthony were in the car.

The next to arrive were the reporter and cameraman from a small news channel that Leo had contacted. He had promised them a big scoop that no one else would have access to. As instructed, they came in their personal car and didn't attract any attention. They stayed hidden as instructed. Leo would call them when it was time.

The GPS tracker on Sinha's SUV showed that it was headed toward the beach house. The plan was a go. Suzanna wore a blond wig and blue contacts and a revealing red bikini under her trench coat. Sinha's GPS position showed that he was twenty minutes away. Leo and Sebastian locked the two cars. Everyone walked over to the side of Sinha's beach house and hid behind the palm trees.

Anna looked extremely nervous, so Sebastian told her, "Don't worry Anna, we will get Anthony in and out really quick and nothing will happen to him. You will be able to see where he is the whole time." Anna held Sebastian's hand and he gave her a reassuring nod.

Sinha's SUV pulled up in front of the beach house. Sinha's bodyguards dropped Sinha at the house and drove away. The beach was deserted as usual. Sinha came out to the patio and set his whiskey bottle on the patio table. He made himself a large drink and sat down on a chair with a smug look on his face. He sipped his drink.

"Action," Leo whispered in Suzanna's ear.

"I had taken acting lessons." She took off her coat and handed it to Leo. "This should be easy." She put on sunglasses and walked out onto the beach. She stopped right in front of Sinha's patio and faced the ocean with her back to Sinha.

Sinha took off his glasses as his jaw fell open when he saw Suzanna in her red bikini. "Excuse me," said Sinha, "who are you?"

Suzanna turned around, acting startled. "Sorry I didn't realize anyone was there. I apologize for obstructing your view."

"I prefer this view any day." Sinha drooled. "Please join me for a drink."

"I would love to." Suzanna walked onto Sinha's patio.

"Please have a seat," said Sinha. "I will make us drinks."

Sinha's phone rang. "Excuse me for a moment," he said.

"Let me make the drinks. You can finish your phone call." Suzanna stood up and took the empty glass from Sinha.

Sinha took a few steps. "Hello, I will not be needing your services today." He paused for a few seconds. "You will still get payment. I will need it for next week. Thanks. Talk to you next week." Sinha hung up.

"Perfect," said Leo. "His pimp isn't going to show up." Fewer people they needed to deal with, the better.

Suzanna made two drinks and added Walt's tranquilizer to Sinha's drink. Sinha took the drink from Suzanna.

"Cheers," said Sinha and raised his glass. "To the most beautiful woman I've ever seen."

"It's Na Zdorovie in Russian." Suzanna raised her glass.

Sinha finished his drink and soon passed out on his chair. Leo came onto the patio and handed Suzanna the coat. "Flawless," said Leo.

"He is disgusting. I could see him look at my breasts the whole time." She removed her wig and put it in the pocket of the trench coat.

"Let's wipe down the glasses and anything you touched for

fingerprints." Leo took out a pair of gloves and some wipes and handed them to Suzanna. She put on the gloves and wiped down everything she had touched. She put on the trench coat and a hat and headed to Leo's car.

Leo put on gloves and carried Sinha into the house. He took off Sinha's shirt and shorts and sat him upright on the bed. Sebastian brought Anthony into the house and sat him next to Sinha on the bed. Anna waited outside because they didn't want her to see her son in this situation. They put on Sinha's sunglasses and placed a selfie stick in his hands. They put a mask on Anthony, so no one would know it was him. They unlocked Sinha's phone using his fingerprint reader and took photos of him sitting with Anthony.

"Do your thing, Walt," Leo said and handed him the phone.

"My pleasure." Walt opened Sinha's email and sent images of Sinha siting with the masked boy to some of Sinha's contacts.

Leo searched through Sinha's briefcase and found 900,000 rupees worth about 13,000 American dollars. He grabbed the cash and put it into his backpack. Sinha was wearing a gold ring with nine diamonds on his finger and a heavy gold chain on his neck. Leo relieved him of both those items.

"He will wake up anytime now. We've got to go," said Walt.

Sebastian unlocked the front door.

Leo made a phone call to the reporter. "If you enter the beach house now, you will get your story. If you don't roll this live, chances are that the crime will be suppressed." Leo hung up the phone. He walked out of the patio as Sinha started to stir.

The reporter and the cameraman burst into the house with the camera rolling live.

"What is going on?" Sinha screamed. "Who the hell are you?" He tried to knock the camera from the cameraman's hands but failed.

The reporter looked at the camera. "We are at the live crime scene where we see this man was about to abuse a young boy. We arrived just in time to save the boy."

Sinha screamed as the police burst into the house.

The reporter stepped aside. "The police are here to arrest this child predator," said the reporter. The cameraman filmed the policemen.

"Arrest him," the inspector shouted, pointing to Sinha. The two constables threw Sinha on the bed and handcuffed him.

Walt had hired local goons to cause a commotion in Sinha's house. These goons were paid handsomely for their cameo in the plan. They were on standby in a van parked a few blocks away from Sinha's house. Walt gave the goons the signal and they stormed into Sinha's house. The demanded to deal with Sinha. The cameraman turned the camera on the goons that were at the doorway. The policemen turned to the mob and tried to calm them down. "Please let us do our job. He will be punished in court." The inspector and the constables were busy dealing with the goons.

During the commotion Sebastian sneaked in through the patio and took Anthony. No one noticed, and by the time the commotion died down, Sebastian was back in the car and Anthony was reunited with Anna. Leo and Sebastian drove to Mumbai. This was the beginning of the end for Sinha.

Anna held her son tight and cried. "You will be able to see and hear soon, my son. I am sorry I had to put you through this. You are safe now." She held Anthony the whole way home.

Leo deposited the cash from Sinha's briefcase into Suzanna's bank account. He dropped her off at the airport the next morning. "You will always have a home in Spain. Adiós mi amor," she said and blew Leo a kiss. It translated to goodbye, my love, in Spanish. Leo watched her walk away until she disappeared into the crowd. He realized that he wouldn't ever see her again.

Sinha made the front page of the local newspapers. The court sentenced Sinha to seven years in a maximum-security prison. The live streaming from the news channel and Sinha's phone were enough for the court to put Sinha behind bars. No one found out the identity of the masked boy. All that mattered was the predator was behind bars.

Isa flew into Mumbai after her two-week trip home. Leo waited at arrivals and picked Isa up. "How was your trip?" asked Leo.

Isa put on her seatbelt. "It was incredible. I needed to spend time with my grandparents." Isa looked relaxed. "Did Mumbai miss me?" asked Isa playfully.

"I have something for you. Open the glove compartment," said Leo.

Isa opened the glove compartment and found a package wrapped in gift paper. She looked at Leo and slowly opened her gift. "A newspaper dated two days ago? Can't say that I have ever received something like this before."

"Open it up," said Leo.

Isa opened the paper and let out a scream. "I can't believe it." On the front page was a picture of Sinha with the caption, "Pedophile arrested." She read the article and wept.

"It's over. He is where he belongs." Leo held Isa's hand.

Leo saw the light in Isa's eyes that he had seen the first time he met her. The darkness had left her. He was drawn to her.

CHAPTER EIGHT

THE DARK PATH

Mumbai, October 2017

Leo and Isa met Sebastian and Walt at a brewery around the corner from their apartment for happy hour. The brewery had recently opened and had become a hotspot because of the live band that played rock music every evening. The master brewer was from Belgium and the beer that the brewery served was heavily influenced by Belgian flavors.

Isa had gone back to her old cheerful self after she learned that Sinha was in jail. Not only did Leo manage to get Isa closure but he also made the first big stride in his journey of taking down criminals.

"There is something I need to tell you." Isa looked at Sebastian first and then at Walt. "I was drugged and attacked by a man named Sinha a few months ago."

Sebastian looked bewildered as he slammed his beer mug on the table, almost breaking it. Walt spat out his beer and swiveled his head to look at Leo. Walt's eyes had become slits on his large face.

Both Sebastian and Walt expected some sort of explanation from Leo.

"I'm sorry guys. It wasn't my place to say anything." Leo put up his hands defensively while shrugging his shoulders. "It needed to come from Isa."

"It's all right, guys. He is in jail now and will be there for a very long time. He can't hurt anyone else." Isa took a sip of her beer.

Walt looked at Leo and shook his head.

Leo took a large gulp of his beer. "We have something important to tell you, Isa."

Isa moved her body to the rhythm of the music.

Leo placed his hand on Isa's. "We were the ones who got Sinha arrested."

Isa frowned. "What do you mean? I thought he was caught red handed." She looked from Leo to Sebastian and Walt.

Sebastian lowered his gaze.

Walt gazed at the band on stage.

Leo explained to Isa how they had entrapped Sinha.

Isa sighed. "I need some air." She got up from her chair and stormed out of the brewery.

"I imagined that conversation going differently," said Walt. He gulped down his beer and refilled his glass from the giant pitcher on the table.

"She needs some time to process everything. She'll come around," said Leo. "We did the right thing."

Isa came back into the brewery shortly and sat down at the table. "What you guys did was wrong, but I am extremely grateful. The bastard got what he deserved." She turned to Sebastian. "I want to meet your girlfriend, Anna, and her heroic son."

"Anna and Anthony would love to meet you," said Sebastian

enthusiastically. "Anthony is getting surgery for his eyes and ears over the next couple of days. We will be able to visit him after his surgeries are done."

"That would be great," said Isa. "I want to thank them for what they did for me. I can only imagine what a tough decision it was for Anna to make."

"To Sinha rotting in jail and to Anthony being able to see and hear." Walt raised his glass. "Cheers."

They wrapped up at the brewery and took the party to Leo's house.

Anthony's surgeries were over, and doctors had cleared him to have visitors. Isa, Leo, and Walt walked into the children's hospital. "We are looking for an eight-year-old boy, Anthony, who had eye and ear surgery. Do you know which room he is in?" Isa asked the young receptionist.

The receptionist smiled. "Anthony is a fighter. Everyone in the hospital knows him." She handed Isa three visitors' passes. "He is in room three twenty-one which is on the third floor."

Isa thanked the receptionist and walked to the elevator with Leo and Walt.

Isa knocked on the door.

Sebastian opened the door and grinned when he saw Isa. "Come on in guys" he said. "Anthony is doing great." Sebastian beamed.

Isa walked in and hugged Anna. "Thanks for what you did, Anna." Isa teared up when she saw Anthony. "How's the little man doing?" Isa asked.

Anna gently stroked Anthony's hair. "He is doing well. He is asleep because of all the painkillers. He cleared all his vision tests and will be able to see. He will need to use hearing aids but will be able to hear. My Anthony will need to go through therapy for a few months, but after that he will be normal like other kids." Anna looked at Anthony lovingly.

Leo wondered how his life would've shaped out if his mother hadn't been taken away from him.

***

Leo started his mornings with a five o'clock run on Marine Drive, a sea-facing promenade that provided an uninterrupted view of the Arabian Sea. He drove to Marine Drive and parked his car. He got out and stared into the ocean while taking deep breaths that filled his lungs with oxygen. He started his run while listening to his classical music mix of Beethoven, Mozart, Vivaldi, and Bach. Leo's father had introduced him to classical music at a young age. Even though Leo had tried to distance himself from everything that reminded him of his father, classical music had stayed with him. The music by legendary composers transported him to a place of peace and transcendence.

After his run, his next stop was the gym where he worked. He did an hour of weight training before starting personal training sessions. Leo's weight training music was hip-hop. The powerful lyrics and infectious beats kept his workout routine upbeat. His father bad-mouthed hip-hop music which was the reason he had started listening to it. After his workout, he took a steam bath and a shower at the gym. He then had breakfast at the gym café, a protein shake and a three-egg omelet.

Leo and Isa were going on their first date later that evening. He checked his watch after each of his sessions. He still had about six hours to go before his date with Isa. Leo wrapped up his sessions and headed home to take a nap. He woke up and got dressed for the date. He knocked on Isa's door, and she opened it. This was the first time Leo had seen Isa dressed up. She wore an elegant dress that hugged her curvaceous body. She took Leo's breath away.

"You can close your mouth now," said Isa as she came out of her apartment and kissed Leo on the cheek.

"You look beautiful." Leo took her arm as they walked toward the elevator. Isa wiped the lipstick marks off Leo's face from where she had kissed him.

Leo had made reservations at a new restaurant and bar. The lower level of the place had an exquisite bar and brewery, and the second level had the first Michelin-star restaurant in India. After parking the car, Leo and Isa walked through the bar to get to the restaurant. "We should hang out at the bar after dinner," said Leo as he checked out the impressive bar.

"I will think about it if the date is interesting." Isa winked.

"I'll try to be the world's most interesting man," said Leo.

Their host showed them to their stylish and private table. Isa was bubbly and cheerful, and Leo loved seeing her that way.

"I am thinking about starting a nonprofit organization to help victims of sexual and domestic violence. It will educate people and potentially save lives. What do you think?" Leo knew the look of determination on Isa's face meant she had made up her mind.

"That's phenomenal, and I would love to be involved. I give self-defense courses at my gym and could help out with something like that." Leo brushed strands of hair off Isa's face.

Leo and Isa split dessert after dinner. As they got up to leave, Leo put his arm around Isa's waist and pulled her close to him. He felt the heat as her body pressed up against his. Isa met Leo's gaze. His touch heightened her senses and caused her moods to dance. He felt her heart flutter and her body quiver against his. He could smell her beautiful scent mixed with the sweet smell of Prosecco she had been drinking. He placed his lips on Isa's and parted her lips gently. Her knees weakened, and her heart palpitated, and her eyes clenched shut when her senses were overpowered. Leo's heart beat hard, as he had never felt such an intimate connection with anyone before. His resolute mouth continued to play with her quivering lips until her body shook. She grabbed onto him from the giddiness that made her head spin. She fell into his arms and held him tight. She rested her head on his chest for a few moments.

Leo and Isa walked down the marble steps leading to the bar below. The chemical reactions in their brains amplified their attraction, and they decided to go back home and explore each other.

As they walked out of the bar, Isa stopped and grabbed Leo's arm. "That woman looks like she's in trouble." She gestured to the bar. A woman who looked intoxicated was surrounded by three men who were being too friendly to her. One of the men offered her a drink, even though she swayed. The second man whispered something to the third man, who took out keys from his pocket and walked toward the exit. It was clear that the men were trying to take advantage of her.

"Those guys are up to no good. We need to help her." Isa walked up to the woman. "Are you okay?"

One of the men stepped forward. "None of your business," he said. He advanced toward Isa menacingly. "Get out of here, or you will regret it."

The second man advanced toward Isa.

Leo stepped in between Isa and the two men. "Let's dance," said Leo, taking off his blazer and laying it on a bar stool. He then took off his watch and put it in his jeans pocket. The look in Leo's eyes and his physique scared the men, and they took off.

"Are you okay?" Isa went up to the woman and put her arm on the woman's shoulder. Isa didn't get a response. "Looks like she is on drugs," said Isa as she saw the glazed look in the woman's eyes. "What did they give you?" She asked.

The woman swayed and looked at Isa with semi-closed eyes. "Coke, cocaine; I want more." The woman slurred.

"Can we drop you home?" Isa sat next to the woman.

"Beach, I want to go to the beach," said the woman, swaying.

"We can't leave her like this. She is in bad shape." Isa looked at Leo. "We need to sober her up and drop her home." Leo agreed and put on his jacket and watch.

"Is her bill paid?" Isa asked the bartender.

The bartender came closer to Isa. "The guys who took off picked up her tab."

Isa thanked the bartender. "Let's take her to the beach and then drop her home," Isa told Leo.

Leo nodded. "She is going to be high for the next six or seven hours," said Leo. "It's going to be a long night."

"We got to her at the right time," said Isa. "If we hadn't checked on her, something terrible could've happened to her."

"Not on your watch, savior of women," Leo said, feeling proud of Isa.

"I can't let anyone go through what I went through. That's all." Isa held the woman who swayed while she walked.

Leo and Isa reached the beach with the woman and sat down on the sand close to the ocean. "Please drink some water." Isa offered the woman a bottle of water.

The woman drank some. The cool ocean breeze seemed to wake

her up as she started talking. "I have been married for eleven years, and I found out today that my husband was cheating on me with my sister." She took another sip of water.

"I am really sorry to hear that. Where do you live?" asked Isa. "We want to get you home safe."

"I work as head of Information Technology for the Royal Global Bank, a bank at Nariman point." The woman slurred.

Isa asked her again where she lived, but all she wanted to do was talk about the bank.

"She doesn't want to be alone. Let's sit with her for a while, and we will take her home when she is ready." Isa was adamant.

"It could be worse, and she could want to go for a swim in the ocean." Leo chuckled.

Isa smacked him on his arm. "She can hear us. She's right here."

Leo threw his arms up.

Cocaine made this woman want to talk about her work life. She talked about the bank and its customers and then went into security details. It was like she drew them a detailed blueprint of the bank. "Most of the clients are politicians and top businessmen, and the bank helps powerful people launder money."

Isa gave her more water.

The lady drank some more water. "The bank keeps a ton of cash and diamonds in the vault."

She now had Leo's attention, and he listened intently.

She took out her phone and showed Leo and Isa pictures and videos of the bank building.

Leo suddenly remembered where he had seen the name Royal Global bank before. He had seen a purple card with the words 'Royal Global Bank platinum member' in Sinha's briefcase the night he had gotten Sinha arrested. A plan formed in Leo's head. Leo transferred pictures and videos from the woman's phone to his while she talked to Isa. Was this a path the universe was showing Leo? Was this his destiny? A random person Leo had met had just given him inside information about a bank he never knew existed, a bank that laundered money for rich and powerful people.

After what seemed like an eternity, the woman regained composure and talked cohesively. Isa handed her the bottle of water. "Could tell us where you live, so we could drop you off?" Isa asked for the sixth time.

After some prodding, she finally gave Leo and Isa her address. Leo and Isa helped her into the back seat of Leo's car. A short ride later, they reached her apartment complex. The woman was passed out, and Isa tried to wake her up. Isa took water out of the bottle and splashed water on her face which caused her to wake up finally. They took her into her apartment and laid her on her couch. Isa wrote her a note letting her know that she was intoxicated and was almost taken forcibly by a few men. Isa made sure to let the woman know that she was safe. Leo and Isa closed the apartment door and headed to Leo's car.

"I thought the note will help her when she wakes up and doesn't remember a thing." Isa put on her seat belt.

"You are a good person." Leo leaned over and kissed Isa on her cheek. "The woman was very lucky you saw her at the bar." Leo started the car.

As they drove home, Leo couldn't stop thinking about all the information the woman had given them.

"You are very quiet, unlike normally," said Isa.

"It's late and I am tired." Leo took Isa's hand into his.

They reached home and decided to call it a night. Later, Leo lay in his bed and stared at the ceiling.

Leo was at the gym the next morning when he got a call from Sebastian. "What's up, brother?" he asked.

"I am in trouble. Need your help." Sebastian was frantic.

"Calm down. Tell me what's going on." Leo walked to a secluded part of the gym.

"I was arrested," said Sebastian, distraught. "Euro Bhai, the owner of the company where I work has been running a car theft ring, and the police arrested him today. They also took a few of us, because they suspect we are in on it." Sebastian was in tears. "My life is over."

"Where are you right now?" asked Leo.

"I am at the police station. I convinced the inspector to let me make one phone call," said Sebastian. "You are my one phone call."

"Stay calm, let me see what I can do." Leo hung up and looked up contact information for criminal lawyers.

After multiple calls, Leo found someone who was available right away and was willing to meet him at the police station. Leo reached the station and tried to meet Sebastian, but the police wouldn't let him. He stood outside the station and waited.

A man in a lawyer's gown pulled into the station riding a motorcycle. "Mr. Das?" Leo walked up to the man.

"Yes, sir," the man said. "Let's go see what we can do about your friend."

"How long have you been a lawyer?" Leo asked. "You look very young."

"Eight days today, sir, and you are my first client." The man smiled.

"No wonder you were the only one who could show up right away and didn't need a retainer," said Leo.

The man grinned sheepishly.

Inside the station, Das transformed from the friendly and awkward person to a man in full control. A short while later, the police released Sebastian. "Wait outside, I will be back shortly," Das told Leo and went back into the station. He came back out looking smug. "We need to go over a few things in my office and settle my payment. Take down my address and meet me there." He gave them his address and got on his motorcycle.

Leo parked the car at the address Das had given them. Leo and Sebastian got out of the car and looked around. "This is a farmer's market, Leo," said Sebastian, sounding surprised.

"Let me call him." Leo called Das. "I don't think you gave me the right address. We are in a market."

"Please walk past the juice shop and turn to your left," said Das.

Confused, Leo and Sebastian walked past the juice bar and turned to their left. They found a little stall with a sign that read D.A.S Law Firm. "Welcome to my office. Please come in." Das beamed.

"Your office is in a market?" Leo shook his head. "Why am I not surprised?"

"Yes, sir," said Das with chuckle. "Three reasons for doing that. One, the rent here is close to nothing and I am worth close to nothing as well. Two, there are three police stations in a three-kilometer radius of this place, and my office is the closest one to all of them. Three, thousands of people who live in the vicinity come here to buy groceries, and I hand out my business card to each one of them. It's great marketing."

"Ingenious," said Leo. "Das, you will make it big time."

"Please step into my office, gentlemen." Das ushered them in.

Das had just enough space for three chairs, a table with a ton of drawers, and a small bookshelf where he kept his law books.

"Thank you for getting me out," said Sebastian.

"Don't thank me yet." He pulled out a piece of paper from his file and waved it at them. "This proves your innocence. Euro Bhai had already confessed to his crime and is going to do a few years in a minimum-security prison. I spoke to him in front of the inspector and got him to sign a document stating that Sebastian had no knowledge of any of the illegal activities happening in the workshop and that he was innocent. I also got two witnesses to sign this letter, and the police will not be coming after you for this crime anymore. Now you can thank me profusely." Das laughed loudly.

Sebastian let out a huge sigh of relief. "Thank you, Mr. Das. I was really scared."

Leo paid Das his well-earned fees and Sebastian filled in paperwork.

Das filed the paperwork. "One other thing, the Euro Motors property is sealed off because it's under active investigation, and you won't be able to get any of your stuff from there until they finish," Das said.

"I live in a small room on the property. What does that mean for me?" Sebastian asked nervously.

"You need to find another place to live until the police wrap up their investigation and clear the property. If you have any friends in need of help, here is my business card." Das handed them a few cards.

"You can stay at my place until you figure things out," said Leo.

"My debt to you keeps increasing," said Sebastian looking worried.

"Don't worry about it. Let's go grab a beer." Leo and Sebastian walked to the car.

"I promise I will pay you back," said Sebastian.

"I'm not worried, I know where you live," said Leo with a wink.

Leo and Sebastian headed to a bar and ordered a couple of cold beers. "I don't know how I am going to pay off all my debts and support my family," Sebastian said. "I am done. Every time I move forward, life fails me. Maybe I should consider going into a life of crime." Sebastian took a large swig of his beer.

Leo had an epiphany. "Isa and I met a woman the other night who works at a bank in Mumbai. She shared inside information about the layout and security of the bank. She also told us about the flaws in the security system."

Sebastian put his beer on the table and stared at Leo in disbelief. "What are you saying?" Sebastian's voice broke.

"I am saying that I want to rob a bank." Leo was calm.

Sebastian put both his hands on his head.

"What do you think?" asked Leo.

Sebastian started to hyperventilate.

"Look, Sebastian, the bank launders money for rich and powerful people. I wouldn't feel bad stealing from it. We will use the money to do good for people in need." Leo ordered another round of beer.

"I don't know if I can survive in jail." Sebastian sighed deeply.

"That's why we need to come up with a foolproof plan. We need to make sure we don't get caught. It is the answer to all your needs."

Sebastian remained silent for a while. "I can't believe I am saying this, but I am in. I don't see any other way for me to support my family and pay of all my debts."

Leo lifted his glass and so did Sebastian.

"I haven't told Isa or Walt anything about this, and we will move forward with this only if they approve," Leo said.

"We should be able to convince Walt easily," said Sebastian. "It's Isa I am worried about."

Leo and Sebastian finished their drinks and headed to Leo's apartment.

A few weeks had gone by and Sebastian spent most of his time in Leo's apartment. He met Anna and Anthony occasionally. Sitting idle bored him out of his mind.

It was the night of Isa's surprise birthday party, and Leo and Sebastian were going to try to convince Isa and Walt to rob the bank. The thought of having a conversation with Isa about robbing a bank made Leo nervous.

Walt arrived at Leo's apartment first, and Leo made him a stiff single malt scotch drink. "This is going to be a good evening," said Walt, holding up his drink.

"Indeed," said Leo, glancing at Sebastian.

Leo decided to be straight up with Walt. "Have a seat." Leo told Walt about the woman Isa and he had met at the bar and the conversation Sebastian and he had weeks earlier.

"I need another drink." Walt got up calmly and went to the bar, where he made another drink. Walt was being too calm. He came back with his drink and sat down.

"Walt, did you hear what I said? The only way we would go through with it is if you and Isa are on board. We will need your expertise to pull off something like this."

"Why do you want to rob a bank?" Walt didn't raise his voice or get agitated.

"Taking Sinha down cost a lot of money but will keep an animal from hurting innocent people. I was able to fund the operation to take Sinha down with the money my mother had left me. I intend to dedicate my life to take down criminals who destroy innocent lives and I need a lot more money to do that. Additionally, Sinha banked at the Royal Global Bank which launders money for criminals. I would have no remorse stealing from an organization that helps criminals." Leo's eyes blazed.

"It's also illegal and could land you in prison," said Sebastian.

"Let your plans be dark and impenetrable as night, and when you move, fall like a thunderbolt," said Walt, sipping on his drink.

"You have a way of making me feel like a moron," said Sebastian shaking his head. "Translation please?"

"It is a quote from Sun Tzu, the strategist and philosopher who lived in ancient China. We need to build a plan that is so effective that it won't land us in prison." Walt took a large gulp of his drink. "This is exactly what I need to break the monotony in my life. I would be honored to join you on this quest for justice."

"No shit, Sherlock." Leo tapped Walt's glass with his.

Things were falling into place. If Leo could convince Isa, they would go through with the plan, the crazy plan that could either give them the opportunity to build a better world or throw them behind bars or end their lives.

After celebrating Isa's birthday, Leo took her to his balcony. The cool ocean breeze blew her luscious hair back from over her face. Leo gazed into Isa's sparkling eyes. "No one makes me feel the way you do." Leo touched Isa's cheek with his thumb.

It was time to have the real conversation with Isa. "The night we met the woman at the bar and took her to the beach, I copied pictures and videos of the Royal Global Bank from her phone to mine." Leo lowered his gaze.

"Why would you do that?" Isa looked puzzled.

"I believe that meeting that woman at the bar was a sign showing us the way to help people in need," said Leo.

"You are still not making sense," said Isa. "A sign telling you to do what, exactly?"

Leo told Isa about the conversation he had with Sebastian and Walt about robbing that bank that laundered money for criminals and using that money to do good deeds.

"Are you insane?" Isa thundered. "That is a criminal offense. What the hell were you guys thinking?" Isa's face turned red.

Leo leaned on the balcony. "Isa, we need to come up with a plan that will work. If all four of us don't agree that it will work, we will walk away. This will be huge for Sebastian, as he will be able to take care of his family. You will be able to start your nonprofit and help countless victims and their families. I intend to take down animals like Sinha, one way or the other."

"That doesn't make it right," said Isa. "Are we going to become criminals?"

"Sometimes we need to think like criminals to take down criminals," said Leo.

Isa stormed out of Leo's apartment. Leo didn't see Isa for a few of days. She didn't pick up Leo's calls or return his text messages.

After days of silence, Leo received a text message from Isa inviting him to dinner that evening at her apartment. Leo was relieved to hear from her.

Leo knocked on the door, and Isa opened it. "Come in" she said.

Leo entered Isa's apartment.

"I haven't been able to sleep properly the last few days. What you told me has really disturbed my mind. I tried as much as possible to justify not agreeing with you. Ultimately, what you guys did for me by taking down Sinha helped me reach my decision. You put in your resources to take down Sinha." Isa came close to Leo. "If you can bring justice to other people like me with money taken from a corrupt organization, I am all for it. I also think I can use money to help countless women across the country who are victims of rape and domestic abuse. I can't believe that I am saying this, but I am in."

Leo hugged Isa tight.

"Also, I'm ready now," Isa whispered into Leo's ear. Those words were music to Leo's ears.

Leo carried Isa into her bedroom and gently placed her on the bed. He got on the bed and placed his mouth on hers. Her trembling lips parted, and his tongue wrestled with hers. His hand reached the zipper on the back of her dress. He undid the zipper and pulled her dress off her body. He felt the heat emanate from her while he ran his hand down her stomach, and she moaned with her eyes closed tight. He ran his lips down her neck and explored her body with his tongue. He went up her inner thigh and pulled down her panties. She arched her back and squealed with desire. He moved his mouth down her toned abs while she quivered and clenched underneath him. He put on the condom he always carried in his wallet and entered her slowly. She moaned loudly as she arched her back and dug her nails into him. As he pushed into her harder and faster, her body contorted, and her eyes rolled into the back of her head. The expressions of agony and pleasure that emanated from her face aroused him more and brought out his primal desire. He exploded into her with a loud, unearthly grunt, and she let out a loud cry of ecstasy as her body quivered and her toes curled. Leo's touch set her nerve endings on fire and her hands had grabbed fistfuls of the bed sheet. Her back was arched high and her mouth open wide. Leo couldn't get enough of her and pushed his body against hers while parting her lips with his. They got to know every emotional and physical pleasure point in each other. The chemical explosions of ecstasy in their brains caused their minds and bodies to become one. They lay sweaty in each other's arms as they waited for their hearts to return to their normal pace.

"I love you," said Isa.

CHAPTER NINE

THE HEIST

Mumbai, December 2017

Now that everyone was on board, they needed a plan. A plan to rob the Royal Global Bank. The information the woman from the bar gave Leo and Isa was critical in formulating the plan. Leo projected on the wall of his apartment the images he had taken from the woman's phone.

"During my research, I found the bank is looking to hire a receptionist," said Walt. He slurped up noodles from a cardboard box using chopsticks.

"Any louder, and the neighbors will hear you." Sebastian shook his head.

"The Japanese believe that slurping noodles brings out more flavor, because you inhale air that enhances the flavor of the noodles." Walt slurped again.

Isa chuckled. "That is great information. About the bank, not about the Japanese slurping their noodles." Isa stood up.

"I am the gift that keeps on giving," said Walt, eating a large chunk of ginger chicken.

"I should apply for the receptionist position, so I can get a good look at the bank. It will be invaluable to have eyes inside the bank," said Isa.

"Brilliant," said Leo. "Let's hope they call you for an interview."

"They will. I will show extraordinary credentials on my application," said Isa.

Isa sent in the job application to the bank under the alias of a Russian student who was pursuing a finance and accounting degree in Mumbai. She came to Leo's apartment one evening. "I got the interview email. It's scheduled for five days from now. I have a few days to work on my Russian image."

"Excellent. The Russian alias will ensure you fly under the radar. They won't be able to tie you to the bank in the future," said Leo.

The morning of the interview, Isa got ready in her bedroom while Leo waited in her living room. "How do I look?" Isa wore a short skirt and tight blouse that hugged her body. With her wig, contact lenses, and glasses, she looked like a completely different person.

"I would like to get to know the Russian you better tonight." Leo winked.

Isa blushed. "Time to attend the interview."

Leo drove Isa to her interview in an untraceable rental car so that he couldn't be tied to the bank. "Be careful, Isa." Leo pulled up to the Royal Global Bank.

Isa got out of the car. One of the armed guards came up to her. The guard told Leo to pull the car around and wait at the parking lot in the back. Leo parked the car in the parking lot behind the building and waited in the car nervously.

A while later, Isa came out of the double doors. Leo let out a sigh of relief.

"How did it go?" Leo opened the passenger door for Isa.

Isa put on her seat belt. "Great," said Isa. "The manager's secretary shared a lot of information with me. Let's go, and I will fill you in."

Leo drove out of the bank gates.

Later that evening, Leo, Isa, Walt, and Sebastian met at Leo's apartment. Isa's firsthand knowledge of the workings of the bank was going to be crucial to the success of their plan.

Leo had set up a white board on his living room wall. "The floor is yours Isa." Leo handed her a marker.

Isa took the marker and drew out the layout. "Once we drove into the gate, we reached the front entrance. There were two armed guards who did basic security checks. Once they were done, I went into the double doors. I walked down a large passageway and reached the reception desk. One man did all the talking, and two heavily armed security guards stood behind him. The man took my cell phone and put it in a large wooden box which he placed on a conveyer belt. Once the man finished security protocols, he pushed a button that opened a door on the wall and gave me access to an elevator. I got in the elevator and reached the lobby. I was welcomed by the manager's secretary, who took me on a tour of the bank. I was amazed at the work that went into the building. They weren't afraid to spend money. I got to spend about ten minutes with the secretary before I met the manager. She was very talkative and gave me a lot of key information about the security protocols. There are two alarm systems in the bank. The first is connected to their wireless network, and the second is connected to their cell phones."

Leo took notes. "Does that mean that if they lose internet and cell phone connectivity, they don't have an alarm system?"

"Correct," said Isa. "The alarm systems that notify the guards downstairs will be disabled if the bank loses cell phone and internet connectivity. Every employee in the bank has access to trigger the alarm system. Once the alarms are disabled, the only way for someone in the bank to contact security downstairs is using walkie-talkies. There are only two walkie-talkies, one of which is with the bank manager, and the second is with the assistant manager." Isa paused to make sure everyone followed.

Walt always had a way to ease the tension in the room. "Did she give you the code to the vault as well?"

"No, smartass, she didn't. The only people who have the code to the vault are the bank manager and the assistant manager. The only entry to the vault is in the manager's office."

Leo took more notes. "This is exactly the info we needed. Your recon is exceptional. Keep going," said Leo.

"The interview with the manager went well. He is sharp and committed to the bank. After the interview, I was escorted to the elevator. When I stepped out of the elevator, I reached a desk exactly like the one where my credentials were checked, and I collected my cell phone. A man stood behind the desk and two heavily armed guards stood behind him. The wooden box that contained my cell phone was laid on the desk. The man behind the desk gave me my phone and said I was good to leave. I walked down a passage to the exit double doors and pushed a button. One of the double doors opened slightly. I pulled it open and shut it behind me. There were two armed guards outside the exit doors. Leo was parked in the parking lot outside the exit doors, and I walked to the car. There is only one gate to enter and exit the bank. That's all I have." The white board was filled with drawings and notes.

"It's almost like you've done this many time before. I am glad you have a degree in architecture." Leo stood up. "The drawing on the board is immaculate. My biggest takeaway is that if we figure out how to disable their internet and cell phone connectivity, we will render them helpless." Leo cracked open a beer.

"If we figure out where their internet cables are, we should be able to destroy them pretty easily. Also, if we get a powerful cell phone jammer and activate it close to the bank, it should take care of their cell phones." Sebastian sounded confident.

"I'm glad that you have that engineering degree." Walt cracked open a cold beer and handed it to Sebastian.

"Almost engineering degree." Sebastian took a large sip.

"Strategy without tactics is the slowest route to victory. Tactics without strategy is the noise before defeat," said Walt.

Sebastian grinned sheepishly. "You called me a smart guy but just made me look stupid. I don't know what the hell your quote means."

Walt grinned. "Not only do we need to carefully build our strategy, but we need to execute it flawlessly."

Leo got up and kissed Isa on the cheek. "Thanks to Isa, we are poised to succeed."

They decided that the heist would happen in two months. There were a lot of pieces that needed to align for their plan to be successful.

"Anyone having second thoughts? Now is the time to back out." Leo looked at each of them.

The plan came together. Leo was the financier of the operation that would cost about five million rupees, about 70,000 American dollars. The big purchases were going to be a beat-up old Yamaha speedboat, an old white van, a powerful cell phone jammer, and best-in-class replica handguns. There were additional small purchases that were integral to the plan as well.

Sebastian, who was the mechanical engineer, was responsible for taking the beat-up old speedboat and modifying it to become the getaway vessel. He was also responsible for the powerful cell phone jammer and for figuring out how to disable the bank's internet connectivity.

Walt was responsible for building a contraption that looked like a tablet with a heavy-duty cover. The device would house chemical gases that could be released by the push of a remote button. The chemicals in the device would knock out people who inhaled them. He was also tasked with building a device that looked like a bomb that could release chemical gas.

Isa and Leo would go into the bank and execute the plan while Sebastian and Walt would be right outside the bank gate running operations.

Leo used connections from his fight nights to get in touch with people in the black market. He spent a significant amount of money but was satisfied with the fake passports that Isa and he would use to gain access to the bank. He was also satisfied with the replica handguns that he bought from the black market. The same person who sold him the passports and guns also sold him a state-of-the-art cell phone jammer.

The big day came way sooner than they expected. Everything was in place for them to succeed. They went over the plan multiple times the night before. Sebastian and Walt stayed in Leo's apartment, and Leo stayed in Isa's apartment.

On the day of the bank robbery, Leo woke up at 4:30 a.m. and drove to marine drive. He put on his classical music mix and started his five-kilometer run. It could be his last run if they got caught, but he would make sure they weren't. Their plan was foolproof. He finished his run and got back to Isa's apartment. He took a cold shower and came out of the bathroom with a towel wrapped around his waist. Isa was asleep. He sat next to her on the bed. It was an hour before sunrise. The light from the twilight sky danced on Isa's skin. Leo caressed her face and ran his thumb across her lips. Isa stirred as she started to wake up.

"It's time," said Leo. "We need to leave in an hour." Isa opened her eyes.

Leo got dressed in his three-piece pinstriped suit and put on his salt-and-pepper wig and facial hair. He also put in his green contacts and transformed himself into Oberoi, the industrialist from London.

Isa put on her three-piece black suit and her black wig, moustache, and beard. She also put on a tweed golf cap and transformed herself into O'Malley, Oberoi's bodyguard. "I'm ready," said Isa.

"Let's do it, O'Malley," said Leo.

Isa tipped her tweed golf cap.

Sebastian and Walt were waiting in Leo's apartment dressed in overalls. The four of them took the elevator down to the lobby and got in Leo's car. The first stop was a parking garage close by where the white van was parked. Sebastian and Walt got into the white van. Leo drove his car out of the parking lot and Sebastian followed him in the white van. The car pulled into the pier. The white van pulled up beside the car.

"Let's load up the boat," said Leo as he got out of his car.

"The dummies are already dressed," said Sebastian. He opened the back of the van where two dummies sat dressed identically to Leo and Isa. There wasn't much activity at the pier, as it was still early. Leo and Sebastian carried the dummies down steps to the Yamaha speedboat moored at the pier. They placed the dummy wearing the same suit as Leo in the driver's seat and the other one in the passenger seat. They covered the dummies with tarp and headed back to the car. Sebastian drove Leo's car to the street closest to the pier and found a parking spot. Leo picked up Sebastian in the van. He put on a Beethoven mix CD and drove toward Nariman Point.

After reviewing the plan and getting the van ready, Leo and Isa waited for their ride to the bank. The white Rolls Royce that Leo had rented with a driver came right on time. As the Rolls Royce entered the gate of the bank, Sebastian parked the van outside the bank on the opposite side of the road.

Sebastian and Walt waited anxiously. "It's been exactly forty-three minutes since Leo and Isa walked in through the double door," said Sebastian as he looked at his watch. "I hope everything is okay."

"I wouldn't panic until the timer hits an hour," Walt said. "Besides, it takes time to load up the suitcase full of money." Walt chuckled.

Sebastian smiled nervously.

Six long minutes later, the elegant Rolls Royce came out of the bank gate. "There is the car," Sebastian yelled. "Do you see them in the car?" He looked through the tinted windows.

"The tint is too dark. Can't see inside." Walt squinted as he tried to look through the tinted windows.

Sebastian put the van in gear and followed the Rolls Royce. "I see Isa's hand outside the window. She is giving us the thumbs up. They did it. We did it!" he yelled as he hit the steering wheel.

The Rolls Royce stopped at the pier and let Leo and Isa out. The driver turned the car around and drove away. Leo held his arm and winced.

Sebastian pulled the white van next to Leo. "Time for the next phase," said Leo.

"He's been shot," said Isa.

Leo looked pale. "I'm okay. We need to finish this."

Leo and Isa changed into overalls in the van and put on hats. Sebastian parked the van behind a large cargo container so that it was out of sight. The four of them headed down the steps to the speedboat. Walt took the tarp off the dummies. Sebastian held a large remote control in his hands. They waited for Sharma, the bank manager to arrive.

Leo saw the bank helicopter circle the pier. "Now," yelled Leo.

Sebastian pushed a button on the remote, and the boat roared to life. Sebastian pulled a lever on the remote, and the boat lunged into the water. The helicopter chased the boat.

"Really glad Sharma took the bait. So far, so good," said Leo.

Sebastian pushed the lever to full throttle, and the boat zoomed forward as its engines roared. The helicopter sped up and closed the gap. Once the boat got close to a huge rock formation, Sebastian maneuvered the remote. The boat swerved and crashed into the rock formation. He hit another button at the same time, which caused the explosives on the boat to go off. The boat blew into smithereens, and debris flew into the water. The helicopter circled the crash site a couple of times and headed back to land.

The four of them had pulled it off. They had created an illusion that the great Houdini would be proud of. They had successfully convinced people that they had died during the getaway. Everything had gone according to plan. They heard police sirens at the pier. Amid all the confusion, police officers walked to the van and dusted it for prints.

Sebastian took out his phone and dialed Anna's number. "Hey, need your help urgently. Leo has been shot. Can't go to a hospital, and need your medical expertise," said Sebastian. "Great, thanks. See you at Leo's apartment. I will text you the address." He hung up the phone. "She is coming with medical supplies, and she will take out the bullet and dress the wound."

Isa held Leo tight. "He's on the verge of passing out," said Isa. "Hang in there, Leo. We are very close to home."

Anna had dressed Leo. Leo lay unconscious on the couch.

Leo regained consciousness and sat upright out of the couch. "What happened?" yelled Leo.

"You passed out. Anna took the bullet out of your arm and dressed the wound. It is going to hurt for a while, but you will be okay," said Isa. She ran her fingers through Leo's hair.

"We did it," yelled Leo. "We got away with it."

"We are all over the news." Sebastian pointed at the television. "Everyone thinks the bank robbers died in the boat crash."

Leo got up from his couch and winced. He walked toward the fridge and took out a bottle of champagne. He handed it to Walt. "Pop this cork as loud as you can."

Walt opened it with a pop. "To pulling off something impossible. We will use the money to make the world a better place. To us." Leo raised his glass and took a large sip.

CHAPTER TEN

INVESTIGATION BUREAU

Mumbai, February 2018

Investigation Bureau was a government-funded organization assigned to cases that were out of the league of the police force. It hired only the best, and anyone who wanted to get selected needed to get through a tough written exam and a tougher physical and psychological exam. The agents who worked in Investigation Bureau sent dangerous criminals to jail or took them out.

A sixty-foot-high perimeter wall mounted with cameras and motion sensors surrounded its two-acre property. Two security guards armed with automatic weapons guarded the only entry and exit point. The building was three floors high with a huge Indian flag waving in front of it. The front door of the building opened onto the second floor where agents and tech geeks sat in their cubicles. Stairs led to the third level and an elevator granted access to the basement. The basement consisted of a forensic lab and a morgue.

The director had an office on the third floor. The third floor also had a conference room with a direct video line to the prime minister of India. The director had served under the prime minister in a covert military special forces group known as The Guardians. The elite group of lethal and highly trained soldiers had performed missions all over Asia, the Middle East, and Africa. The director was a sniper and was known fondly as Eagle, because he held the record for the longest kill shot. After twenty-five years of serving their country, The Guardians had retired. Investigation Bureau was the brain child of the director and the prime minister.

The director walked into the conference room on the third floor. "Good morning Zubaria. Are you ready for this?"

The young woman who wore a black suit stood up. "I think so, sir." The director motioned for her to sit down. "Thanks for sitting through this with me, director," said Zubaria.

The director sat down beside Zubaria. "The guys from internal affairs can be pushy. You acted in self-defense. I just want to make sure they know who the real hero is."

Zubaria, the lead field agent, was also the youngest. Her father had served in the Indian Army and had lost his life behind enemy lines. Her mother was a refugee from Pakistan who was given asylum in India as part of the program protecting Christians who were being persecuted. Zubaria had completed a criminal justice degree at Pennsylvania State University in Philadelphia with a full scholarship. While she was in law school at Yale University in Connecticut, her mother was murdered in India for being at the wrong place at the wrong time. She returned for her mother's funeral and decided to stay. She joined Investigation Bureau to help clean up the streets of India.

The door to the conference room opened and the director's administrative assistant showed in two men dressed in suits. "Director, internal affairs are here."

The director thanked his assistant who closed the conference room door. "Good morning, gentlemen. Welcome to Investigation Bureau." The director stood up and shook hands with the two men.

The men in suits shook hands with Zubaria. "This should be relatively painless," one of the men said.

Zubaria nodded.

The second man took out his tablet. "The reason we are having this conversation is because the doctor, the man who kidnapped you, is dead," the second man said. Both had their tablets open. One of the men placed a video camera on the table and pointed it at Zubaria.

"He was no man. He was an animal," said the director. "He brutally murdered many women."

One of the men turned on the video camera. "Agent Zubaria, please walk us through the orchid killer case."

Zubaria took a deep breath and started. "The police had investigated the orchid killer case for a few years and hadn't made any progress. It was assigned to Investigation Bureau, and the director assigned me to the case a few months ago. The killer had already tortured and killed thirteen women. Every woman who died at his hands was found with their arms crossed over their chests and with an orchid placed on their mouths. I chased the killer for two months and didn't get anywhere. One night I found a discrepancy in the doctor's report on one of the victims. I called the doctor who had been helping with the case. He invited me over to his farmhouse where he lived with his wife and three children. We discussed the report and I thanked him and drove out of the farmhouse. Something didn't seem right about the doctor. I parked my car outside the gate and walked back in with my gun and flashlight to look around the farmhouse. I felt a prick on my neck and collapsed before I could react. I woke up in a small dimly lit room where I was tethered to the wall with a rope long enough to get me to every corner of the room. I found a slit in the door and yelled to see if anyone else was there. I saw many rooms just like mine through the slit. I heard muffled crying and realized there were others. A woman's voice told me that she had been there for what seemed like weeks. Unknown to the doctor's family, he had a secret life as a serial killer. The effects of the drugs started to wear off, and I composed myself. I ripped out a piece of wood from my bed and hid it under my shirt. The doctor came into my cell visibly upset. He told me that I had ruined his plans. He said he had made the mistake of kidnapping an officer of the law and he didn't have a choice but to kill me. He had a gun in his hand and paced the room. When he turned, I lunged at him and plunged the sharp piece of wood into his neck, severing his jugular. He went down screaming and held his neck as he bled out. He lay motionless on the ground as I searched him. I found a blade on him, which I used to cut through the rope that tethered me. I went up to the house and called the director. The orchid killer bled to death. That's how it happened." Zubaria took a deep breath and drank water.

The second man turned off the camera. "Thank you for the detailed information. Seems straightforward to me," said one of the men wearing a suit. "Clear case of self-defense. He would've killed you if you hadn't acted."

The director's chest swelled with pride. "Gentlemen, she is a hero. She saved the lives of the six women who were in the doctor's farmhouse and maybe many more. She is law enforcement's finest."

The man who operated the camera put it back in his bag. "I am sorry that we made you relive all that. Unfortunately, it's protocol. Off the record, the sick bastard deserved what he got. In my eyes, you did society a huge favor."

The second man chimed in. "Off the record, I am glad the psychopath is dead. Wish he had died a slower death though."

"My thoughts exactly." The director stood up. "Thank you, gentlemen." The men shook his hands and left.

"That went well," said Zubaria. "Thought it was going to be more painful."

"There are some good ones in internal affairs," said the director. "I am proud of you." The director placed his hand on her shoulder.

The director's phone beeped. "The prime minister wants to chat now." He turned on the video conference device in the room.

Zubaria got up to leave. "I will leave you to it."

"Stay. I think the prime minster would like to thank you for what you did," said the director.

The video equipment beeped, and the prime minister's upper body filled up the large screen. "How are you, Eagle, my old friend?" The prime minister asked.

"I am keeping busy, sir," the director responded.

"I heard that your team took down the orchid killer." The prime minister sipped on a cup of tea.

"Sir, I want to introduce you to the agent who closed the case. This is Zubaria, our youngest agent." The director guided Zubaria to the front of the screen.

"Well done, Zubaria. You have made your country proud. Keep up the great work." The prime minster applauded.

"Thank you, prime minister. It's an honor to meet you," said Zubaria.

"The honor is mine," said the prime minister. "Eagle, the reason for the call is because there has been a bank robbery. Some of the members of my political party bank there and I told them that I would ask you to help. The Royal Global Bank was robbed a short while ago, and my phone hasn't stopped ringing."

"We will investigate, sir. Zubaria will take lead," said the director.

"Thanks, Eagle. Good luck." The prime minister's screen went blank.

Zubaria put on her shoulder holster and holstered a gleaming Glock 19 on each side. She then put on a jacket and got in her jeep. She drove to the pier where the bank robbers had orchestrated their getaway. There were a few police vehicles when she got there. She parked her car and walked to the boat dock.

"Looks like you have lost your way, madam, there aren't any bars and clubs around here," a policeman yelled out. He looked at his fellow policeman and both snickered.

Zubaria walked up to the policeman who had made the comment and looked him up and down. "When I got out of my jeep and saw you from about a hundred feet away, I wondered why a woman this close to delivering her baby was on duty. As I got closer, I realized that you are just someone who gave up trying. Your fat belly looks like it's trying to rip out of your uniform shirt and escape. The buttons on the shirt are doing an unbelievable job of holding your belly in."

The man's mouth dropped as his fellow policeman burst out laughing.

"How dare you talk to a policeman like that?" He moved menacingly toward her.

"The speed at which you move must make you a favorite among criminals," said Zubaria. "They wouldn't need to run; they could just jog away."

The fellow police officer laughed again.

When Zubaria looked at him sternly, he went silent. She took out her ID and flashed it at the two men. "Call the officer in charge of this investigation and let him or her know that I will be taking charge," said Zubaria.

The two policemen jumped up and saluted her, apologizing profusely.

The policeman with the fat belly brought the inspector in charge over. He shook her hands.

Zubaria looked around. "What are your findings?"

The inspector took out his notepad. "We took a statement from the bank manager." He filled Zubaria in on the getaway boat crash. "We discovered a white van abandoned in the pier and have dusted it for fingerprints. It has been completely wiped down," said the officer.

"What about the site of the crash?" asked Zubaria.

"All we could find were bits and pieces of the boat floating on the water. Most of it sank into the ocean. I guess karma caught up with the bank robbers and took them to the depths of the ocean," said the inspector.

"Is the bank manager still around? I would like to ask him a few questions," said Zubaria.

"Yes, madam," said the inspector pointing to the manager.

Zubaria questioned the manager about the incidents that transpired earlier that morning. "One last question. How did you know the bank robbers were going to the marina?"

"Just before they locked me inside the vault, I overheard one of them say that they needed to get to the marina immediately or they would miss their boat," said the manager.

Zubaria took notes in her book and wondered if the thieves had intentionally let slip that they were going on a boat or had made a mistake that caused them their lives.

She went to the inspector and told him that she wanted to go to the crash site.

The inspector motioned to two of his men. "Anything you need madam," said the inspector. He asked the men to take Zubaria to the crash site.

Zubaria reached the huge rock formation and saw that the crash had done a lot of damage. Portions of the rock were charred. "Please collect the pieces of debris." Zubaria pointed at pieces of debris floating in the water. The two policemen collected the pieces. "Please anchor the boat." She jumped onto the rock formation. She put on her gloves and took plastic sample bags from her jacket pocket. She moved around the rock and found additional pieces of charred debris. She took a final look around and took a few pictures. She hopped back into the boat.

When she reached the dock, only a couple of policemen remained. She called one of them over and asked him to get the van delivered to Investigation Bureau. She then drove to her office.

When she entered the lab, a young woman with short black hair wearing glasses came up to Zubaria and hugged her. "Hey Ava, we've got some analyzing to do."

Ava, one of the top forensic scientists in the country, ran the lab.

"Anything for you Zub," Ava said flirtatiously.

"New tattoo?" asked Zubaria, pointing to the back of Ava's neck.

"Yeah," said Ava and her eyes twinkled. "It's an orchid, because we took down the orchid killer." She beamed.

"That's dark, even for you, Ava," said Zubaria.

She walked Ava through the bank robbery and the boat crash during the getaway. She handed Ava the bags of debris.

"What am I looking for?" asked Ava.

"I'll take anything you give me," said Zubaria. "I am having all the evidence shipped to you."

"Of course," said Ava. "You want to grab a drink tonight?"

"Absolutely," said Zubaria. She headed back to her desk.

That evening Ava and Zubaria went to a little bar close to their office to grab dinner and drinks. "I love the fact that we can put the animals that commit such atrocities where they belong," said Ava.

"Amen, sister, either in prison or under the ground," said Zubaria, raising her Martini.

"I like that, Zub," said Ava. "I will use that in my autobiography someday."

Zubaria chuckled.

"You find anything on the bank robbery case?" Zubaria took a sip of her martini.

"Indeed," said Ava. "There are a few things that I discovered."

"Enlighten me," said Zubaria.

"All the debris was fiberglass or metal consistent with materials a speedboat is made of," said Ava. "What was strange was that some pieces of debris showed traces of explosives."

"Interesting," said Zubaria. "That's great information. There are a few things that don't make sense."

"What are you thinking?" asked Ava eating the olive from her martini.

"When the bank robbers were locking the manager in the vault, he overheard them say they were headed to the marina. That's how he knew that the robbers were headed to the marina. Why would they let slip that information? Why would they say that they were going to miss their boat? The only passengers on the boat were the bank robbers. It just doesn't sit right." Zubaria stared at her plate for a few seconds before opening her eyes wide.

"I know that look. You are about to tell me something that's going to blow my mind." Ava sounded like an excited child.

"Could someone control the boat from land? The boat collided into the rocks about a kilometer into the water. Could someone build a remote control with that kind of range?" Zubaria's mind raced.

"With the right person and tools, it absolutely could be done. There are remote control devices with much longer ranges out there." Ava waited for the next words to come out of Zubaria's mouth.

"Well Ava, my darling, I think we are dealing with a group of tech savvy and methodical people. More than likely highly educated. Based on everything I have heard and seen, I am going to say that our bank robbers pulled off the ultimate illusion. I think they got the bank manager to go to the pier and then blew up the boat right in front of his eyes. There would be no question in his mind that the robbers died while making their getaway."

Ava got up and hugged Zubaria. "Brilliant. No wonder the prime minister called us. The police wouldn't have been able to figure it out." Ava lifted her martini. "To brilliant minds." She gulped down the rest of her drink and motioned for the waitress to bring two more.

"The one thing they didn't count on was that we have the most brilliant forensic scientist in the country," said Zubaria.

Ava blushed.

After dinner they headed back to the apartment complex where both lived.

"Do you want to come to my place for a bit?" Ava held Zubaria's hand as the elevator stopped at Ava's floor.

"I can't. I will see you bright and early tomorrow morning." Ava kissed Zubaria on the cheek and walked out of the elevator.

As Zubaria stood under the shower, she could not help feeling a sense of admiration for the people who had pulled off the ultimate deception. She would continue her investigation but let the bank robbers think the case was closed.

CHAPTER ELEVEN

THE INVESTIGATION

Mumbai, March 2018

Zubaria reached the office early the next morning and brewed her coffee. She started her mornings at work with a cup of Turkish coffee. She had been introduced to it by her Turkish college roommate in the US. She drank her coffee and organized her thoughts before her meeting with the director.

Ava came to the office shortly and stopped by Zubaria's desk. "Do you know how Moses makes his coffee?" Asked Ava.

"Moses who?" Zubaria asked.

"Moses, from the Ten Commandments," said Ava as she sat on Zubaria's desk.

"I don't," said Zubaria, browsing through the file she held.

"He brews it. Get it? Hebrews it." Ava chuckled.

Zubaria shook her head. "Hilarious."

"I will leave you to it." Ava walked to the elevator and disappeared into it.

The director walked in twenty minutes later and headed up the stairs to his office. He settled in and called Zubaria. She went up the stairs and was ushered in by the director's administrative assistant.

The director pointed to a chair across from his desk. "Come on in and have a seat. Fill me in on the information we have about the bank case."

Zubaria took a seat. "I interviewed the bank manager and staff at the bank. The thieves walked in dressed as businessmen from London. Their passports and fake cash were impeccable because security didn't flag them. They had inside information about the bank because they knew exactly how to disable the alarm systems and render the bank vulnerable. They apparently used a cell phone jammer and must have cut the fiber optic cables leaving the bank without any connectivity to security. They were in and out of the bank with cash and diamonds in less than an hour." Zubaria leaned back in her chair and paused so that the director could assimilate the information. "I believe that we are dealing with a smart and technology savvy group of people who have managed to create the ultimate illusion."

The director took off his glasses and placed them on the table. "Why did you say it was an illusion?"

"I believe the people who did this are very much alive. They wanted to close the investigation before it even started." Zubaria leaned forward in her chair and explained her theory to the director. "I think we should keep this information confidential. It could give us the element of surprise."

"Impressive." The director looked at Zubaria thoughtfully. "They didn't count on the fact that this case would get assigned to us," said the director. "They had inside information about the bank, which leads me to believe that they either worked there or knew someone who did. Let's keep the fact that we are still investigating the case under wraps. Too bad that these guys are on the wrong side of the law." The director stood up and put on his glasses. "I will keep the prime minister informed. Keep me in the loop on any developments. You are dismissed."

"Thank you, sir. Will do." Zubaria walked out of the director's office and headed down to her cubicle.

Zubaria got in her jeep and headed to the Royal Global Bank. She was met by the bank manager at the front door. "Hello, special agent," said the bank manager with a frown on his face. "I thought this is an open-and-shut case. Why the investigation?"

Zubaria took off her sunglasses. "The case is open until I shut it. I am here to do my job. Is that going to be a problem?"

"No problem. Please follow me," said the bank manager, walking to the double doors. One of the security guards opened the double doors, and Zubaria followed the manager inside. "The security desk where credentials are validated, and weapons and any communication devices are collected from customers," said the bank manager, walking down the passageway. He stopped at the reception desk at the end of the long passageway.

Zubaria held up her badge.

The man behind the reception desk looked carefully at her badge. "Hello, special agent," he said.

"I am here to investigate the robbery that took place at the bank. I am going to record our conversation, so I can go through it later," said Zubaria. "Walk me through the events that transpired on the day of the robbery." Zubaria took out a recording device from her jacket pocket and turned it on.

The man walked her through everything that happened on the day of the heist.

"Thank you. That's all I have for this group." Zubaria said to the manager. "Are they statues?" asked Zubaria, pointing to the two giant mercenaries with weapons standing behind him. "They haven't moved since I got here."

"We get that a lot," said the man behind the desk. "They move only when it is required."

The manager got into the elevator, and Zubaria followed. A short ride later the elevator doors opened to the entrance of the main lobby. The receptionist welcomed Zubaria with a smile.

Zubaria's jaw dropped when she saw the main lobby. "This is incredible. It's like being in the Sistine Chapel." Zubaria stopped and admired the ceiling.

"Under other circumstances, I would've given you the tour," said the bank manager. "It's terrible that we were breached." He paused for a few moments as Zubaria continued to appreciate the ceiling. "Whenever you are ready, please follow me to my office."

Zubaria looked around the room and followed the manager into his office. "Nice view," she said, walking to the window overlooking the ocean.

"Thank you. Can I get you something to drink?" The manager sat on his chair.

"Won't be necessary. What I need is to do is talk to anyone who interacted with the thieves that day." Zubaria sat down on the plush leather chair across from the manager. "I will also need a list of anyone out of the ordinary who had access to the bank."

Zubaria turned on her recording device. "Walk me through the events that transpired on the day of the heist." She placed the recording device on the manager's desk.

The manager walked her through everything that had happened. "I am glad that they are dead. We are not too concerned about the assets that were stolen, it's our reputation that we are concerned about." The bank manager loosened his tie. "The thieves have exposed a major flaw in our security system and we are addressing it."

Zubaria turned off the recording device. "I would like to speak to your secretary and the receptionist. Do you have video footage of the people entering and leaving the bank?" Zubaria took the device and placed it in her jacket pocket.

"We have video recordings that are backed up for six months and then erased. The receptionist wasn't here when the robbery occurred. She won't be able to tell you anything." The manager picked up his phone.

"That's interesting. Who was the receptionist before that?" Zubaria leaned forward in her seat.

"The receptionist before that got married and moved to Delhi. We interviewed several candidates for the position, and they all got a tour of the bank. They wouldn't have known about our security systems, though. They were the only people who were not regulars to enter the bank." He spoke into the phone, telling his secretary to come in.

"I will need footage of all the people who came in for the interview," said Zubaria. "One of them could be how they got eyes into the bank. What about a cleaning crew?"

The manager's secretary came into the office.

"We have been working with a cleaning company since we first opened, and they come in after business hours through our service entrance, and our security guards supervise them," said the manager.

"I would like the name of the company, so I can talk to them." Zubaria stood up.

"Of course. We will provide any information you need." The manager addressed his secretary. "The special agent would like to talk to you."

"Please follow me," said the secretary. "We can use the conference room to talk." Zubaria thanked the bank manager and followed the secretary.

Zubaria sat in the conference room and asked the secretary to sit across from her. "I am going to record our conversation."

The secretary looked nervous. She walked Zubaria through the events that occurred the day of the heist. "What about the people who came in for the interviews? Do you remember anything about them that seemed out of the ordinary?"

"They were all women in their twenties and came in for the interview and left," said the secretary.

"Did you give them tours of the bank?" Zubaria asked.

"Yes, I did." She went red suddenly. She stared at the recording device and buried her face in her hands.

Zubaria turned off the recording device. "Relax, I have turned the device off. What happened?" Zubaria walked around the table and leaned on it. She placed her hand on the secretary's shoulder. "It's okay. You can talk to me."

The secretary gained composure. "I just remembered that one of the women who came in for the interview was a Russian student called Katya Zhirkov. She asked a lot of questions about the security protocols of the bank. She was very friendly, and I told her how the security systems worked. If the manager finds out, I will lose my job." She looked at Zubaria and tears welled up in her eyes.

"Don't worry, I am not going to tell anyone what you told me. You just gave me a big lead in the case. Wipe your tears and go about your life just like normal. You will be okay." Zubaria headed back to the manager's office before leaving the bank. The manager gave her information about the candidates the bank had interviewed and video footage from the days of the interviews. He also handed

Zubaria video footage of the day of the heist. Zubaria thanked the manager and left the bank.

Zubaria drove to Investigation Bureau and went to her desk. She went down the list of candidates who had interviewed for the receptionist position at the bank. The first person she called was Katya Zhirkov. The number was invalid. She contacted the college listed on Katya's resume. The college that Katya claimed she was enrolled in a finance program didn't have a record of her.

Zubaria took the elevator down to the lab and entered double sliding doors. There were three sections in the basement. The first was the forensic lab, Ava's universe, where Ava did her magic. Five small rooms where case evidence was mapped were part of Ava's universe. The second part of the basement was the morgue and autopsy area, which Ava called the death pit. She tried to stay out of the death pit unless it was necessary. The third was a server room that held all information about Investigation Bureau. There was a small office attached to the server room where a skinny man with thick glasses and intense eyes sat by himself.

Ava beamed as Zubaria walked in to the lab. "Welcome to my universe, love. How'd your meeting with the director go?" She gave Zubaria a warm hug.

"You give the best hugs." Zubaria smiled warmly. "Meeting was good. We've got a lot of work to do."

"Only for you, my darling." Ava blushed.

Zubaria reserved one of the war rooms by writing her name down on a board outside the door. "Ready, Ava?" Zubaria waved to the man in the server room. "Hey, Geeky, how are you doing?"

The man waved back. "Good Zub." Geeky smiled and adjusted his glasses. He saw Ava and turned bright red.

Zubaria looked at Ava with mischief in her eyes.

Ava rolled her eyes.

"The man is in love with you, Ava. He literally goes red and becomes speechless every time he sees you." Zubaria walked into the war room, and Ava followed.

"Well, he knows very well that I play for the other team. Besides, he's like a male version of me. Even if I was into guys, he wouldn't be my type. My type would be the exact opposite of me." Ava took a seat on one of the chairs surrounding the rectangular desk.

"Okay, let's get to it." Zubaria dimmed the lights in the room and switched on the projector. It buzzed and came to life. The wall lit up and showed Investigation Bureau logo.

"I'm surprised we are dealing with a robbery case." Ava navigated the equipment using a wireless mouse and keyboard. The wall now showed folders of all the active cases.

"Special request from the prime minister," said Zubaria, looking intently at the wall.

Ava opened the folder that held files related to the bank robbery case. "Are you able to check if a Russian citizen is in the country based on a name?" Zubaria asked.

"Of course." Ava pulled up a database on her computer and worked her magic. The computer buzzed for a while before it beeped loudly. The words not found in red appeared on the wall. "No one by the name Katya Zhirkov in the country." Ava pulled up the video footage from the day of the robbery that showed Leo and Isa in their disguises. "I am going to run a facial recognition program on Katya Zhirkov to see if she matches either Oberoi or O'Malley. This should be done shortly." As she ran the software, the computer beeped several times. "Voila. Katya and O'Malley are the same person." Ava's eyes twinkled.

"Fantastic work, Ava." Zubaria got up from her chair and walked to the wall where the images were projected. "Hello, suspect one. A female suspect. There were two people in the bank and I would imagine at least one or two more on the outside who were in the white van." Zubaria's mind raced. "What would you do, Ava, if you successfully managed to steal money and diamonds from a bank?" Zubaria turned to look at Ava.

"I would lie low for a while and find someone on the black market capable of buying and selling diamonds. I would also find someone who could swap out the marked bills for unmarked bills." Ava's eyes twinkled.

"Precisely. None of the reputed jewelers will touch the diamonds because they are certified and have serial numbers. They would have to find someone on the black market. I will work with my contacts to figure out who can move diamonds and cash. We will get them. It's only a matter of time. What about the van?" Zubaria put on her jacket.

"Van was wiped clean. No fingerprints or DNA. No evidence," said Ava.

"They used a sophisticated device with chemicals and they also built a remote-controlled boat. Someone on their team knew their way around chemicals and mechanical devices. Good info for a day's work." She kissed Ava on the head.

"Dinner tonight?" asked Ava. "I am cooking Mediterranean food."

"Sounds like a plan," said Zubaria. "I'll bring Wine."

Zubaria sat at her desk. She called a few of her sources and compiled a list of five of the biggest players on the black market. She then headed to the director's office. She briefed the director on everything she knew about the case.

"You have accomplished a lot in a day," said the director looking impressed.

"We still have a lot of work to do," said Zubaria.

The director leaned forward in his chair. "Any resources you need. I know this is not our typical case, but this will be a big one."

Zubaria pulled up a document on her phone. "I have found five black-market players who can move the kind of volumes of cash and diamonds that was stolen. I am going to request surveillance on them. It's a long shot, but I think that once the media attention blows over, the bank robbers may try to move the stolen property through one of the black-market players."

The director stood up. "I will get you resources for surveillance. Anything else?"

"No sir, that's it for now." Zubaria stood up.

"Dismissed," said the director.

Zubaria walked out.

Later that evening, Zubaria rang the doorbell at Ava's apartment.

Ava stood at the door wearing an apron and a large smile. "Welcome."

Zubaria held up two bottles of wine. "Smells amazing," said Zubaria as she walked into Ava's apartment. She placed the bottles of wine on the dining table. "I could use a drink." Zubaria uncorked a bottle of red wine and poured two glasses.

"Once we solve this case, I will get a tattoo of one of the lions from the bank on my shoulder," said Ava, pointing out one of the few spots that she didn't already have a tattoo.

Zubaria shook her head. "You are addicted to tattoos." She raised her glass. "To solving the Royal Global Bank heist."

"To solving the heist and me getting a new tattoo." Ava raised her glass.

Zubaria chuckled.

Ava took a sip of her wine and smacked her lips. "I am going home in a few weeks to visit my family. Do you think you can drop me off at the airport?"

"Of course, how long are you gone for?" Zubaria took a chip and dipped it in the hummus that Ava had made.

"Just for a week. Don't miss me too much." Ava winked.

"The hummus is delicious. You know that I will miss you. I am glad you get to spend time with your family." Zubaria ate another crunchy chip dipped in hummus.

After eating Ava's delicious cooking and drinking two bottles of wine, Zubaria headed back to her apartment. She put her head on the pillow and stared at the ceiling. "We are going to get you very soon." She was asleep moments later.

CHAPTER TWELVE

DESTINY'S INTERVENTION

Mumbai, May 2018

It had been a couple of months since the heist, and media attention started to blow over. Leo planned to wait a few more weeks before selling the diamonds on the black market and moving the marked cash through a money launderer in Mumbai. Isa had graduated with her music degree and was involved in launching her nonprofit organization.

The morning of the inauguration of Aashray, Isa's nonprofit organization, was upon her. Aashray, which translated to shelter, would serve as a safe haven for victims of abuse. The inspector who had helped Isa during her legal battle against Sinha was the chief guest. The inspector, Kajal, her lawyer from the Sinha trial, and the counselor who had helped her through her ordeal were going to be board members. The inspector helped Isa lease an abandoned school building outside of Mumbai that had been seized by the police many years earlier. Isa renovated the building and it became her headquarters. Leo was a board member of Aashray and the financier as well. He poured in everything he had left into Aashray. Leo's bank account was almost empty, but he would be swimming in money soon.

Leo woke up early and drove to Marine Drive and went on his run. When he got back to the apartment, the sun was just beginning to rise, and Isa was asleep. He took a shower and got ready for Isa's big day.

"What time is it?" Isa's muffled voice asked from under the blanket.

"Good morning, sunshine, it's after six thirty." Leo walked over to Isa and gently pulled her blanket down.

Isa squinted as her eyes got used to the light coming in from the window. "I'm up," said Isa. She pulled her hair back into a bun and sat on the bed.

"We have to leave in thirty." Leo kissed Isa on the forehead. "Coffee?"

"Thanks, baby." Isa blushed. "That's the first time I've ever called you that." She disappeared into the bathroom.

"I like the sound of that." Leo smiled as he walked to the kitchen to brew coffee.

Isa came out of the bedroom ready to go. "I'm ready."

Leo handed her a cup of coffee. "Coffee to go." Leo kissed Isa on the lips. "I'm really proud of what you are doing. You are going change people's lives for the better."

"I love you." Isa kissed Leo and held him tight. "Let's go."

Leo and Isa took the elevator to the lobby.

Isa and Leo wore purple polo shirts with pink lotuses etched on them that Isa had had designed. Below the lotus was the word Aashray. All board members and volunteers at the inauguration event would be wearing the purple polos as well. Isa had chosen purple because it combined the calmness of blue and the fire of red. The lotus symbolized purity and self-regeneration.

Sebastian and Walt waited in the lobby. The elevator doors opened, and Leo and Isa came to the lobby sipping coffee.

"What's with the dark shades?" Leo asked Walt, punching him in the arm lightly. "You are inside a building."

"The man was up until three a.m. drinking beer. He has bags under his eyes." Sebastian shook his head.

"Need some greasy food and a soda. Can we pick something up on the way?" Walt grunted.

"Breakfast of champions," Leo said with a chuckle. "We have to pick up the flowers on the way. There is a bakery next door, and I'll pick up something to eat. Something extra greasy for you." Leo pointed at Walt.

"My man," said Walt with a huge smile.

Leo drove in the direction of the Aashray headquarters. He stopped on the way by the florist. "Let's go. While you pick up the flowers, I will get some food." Leo left the air conditioner running.

Leo went into the bakery while Isa headed to the flower shop. Leo came out of the bakery with a brown paper bag and walked to the florist.

Isa was at the florist waiting for the bouquets she had ordered. A middle-aged woman came up to Isa and tapped her on the shoulder. Isa turned around, and the woman teared up.

The woman pulled out a handkerchief and wiped her tears. "I'm really sorry."

Isa put her hand on the woman's shoulder. "Do I know you? Are you okay?"

The woman hugged Isa. "I'm sorry for what my husband did to you."

"Your husband?" Isa was puzzled.

"Raj Sinha was my husband. I didn't know what a monster my

husband was. He got what he deserved. My daughters and I have cut all ties with him and his family. We have given up his name as well." The lady wiped her tears.

Thoughts of Sinha and the courtroom flashed in Isa's mind. She hadn't thought about what Sinha had done to her in a while. "It's not your fault. He is where he needs to be, and he can't harm anyone else. I hope Arya is practicing music. She has real talent."

"She is very withdrawn these days and spends a lot of time immersed in music," said the woman.

Isa took the woman's hand. "Please give Arya my best wishes. She is very talented and is destined to do big things."

The woman placed her hand on Isa's cheek. "God bless you." She turned around and left.

Leo heard the last part of the conversation. "You okay?" He put his arm around Isa's waist.

"Haven't thought about the incident with Sinha in a while," said Isa.

The woman at the checkout counter placed three bouquets in front of Isa.

Isa paid and took the bouquets. "I'm okay. Let's do this."

Leo pulled into the school gate and was welcomed by volunteers in their purple polo shirts. The volunteers had gone all out with public relations and the turnout at the inauguration was higher than expected.

The inspector, who was in uniform, gave a powerful speech that explained the significance of what Isa was doing. The inauguration was official when the inspector lit a lamp and cut a red ribbon outside the front door of the building. Aashray would make a difference in the lives of many victims of abuse and give them courage, strength, knowledge, and a safe haven.

The inspector's phone rang. "Excuse me." The inspector stepped away. "Hello, commissioner, what can I do for you?" She moved a few feet away and stood under a tree.

Leo walked up to the inspector with a glass of freshly squeezed lemonade and overheard her conversation on the phone.

The inspector raised her voice. "What? Investigation Bureau thinks the bank robbers are still alive?"

Leo froze. He ducked behind the tree and listened intently.

"Understood, sir. I will get right on it." The inspector hung up the phone.

Leo's heart raced.

The inspector went up to Isa. "Something important has come up, and I need to take care of it. I will catch you later. You are a hero, and we need more people like you." The inspector climbed into her jeep and drove away.

Leo walked up to Isa. "We need to find Sebastian and Walt. I need to talk to you all urgently." Isa followed Leo.

Sebastian sat under a tree sipping on a bottle of Thumbs Up, a fizzier and spicier version of Coca-Cola.

"Walt, we need to talk now," said Leo, grabbing his arm. Walt groaned and stood up slowly.

Sebastian stood near the front gate of the school and talked into his phone. Leo walked up to him and motioned for him to hang up. "Need to talk urgently."

Sebastian told his mother that he would call back later and hung up. "What's going on?"

"Follow me." Leo went to where Isa and Walt waited. "We need privacy." He went into a classroom in a corner of the school, and the others followed. Leo closed the door once everyone was inside.

Isa took Leo's hand. "You are acting strange. What's going on?"

Leo took a deep breath. "I was taking lemonade to the inspector when I overheard her on the phone." He got puzzled looks from Walt and Sebastian. "They know. They know we are alive."

Walt spit out the soda.

Sebastian shrieked. "I can't go to jail. I won't survive in jail."

Leo put his arms around Sebastian's shoulders. "No one is going to jail. We'll figure this out. I don't think the police know anything else besides the fact that the bank robbers are alive. We are going to lay low for some more time. Just go about your lives as normal." He took Isa's hand.

Isa squeezed Leo's hand. Leo looked her in the eye and mouthed the words, "I'm sorry."

***

Sebastian went home for a week for his sister's wedding and was on his way back to Mumbai. Walt would pick Sebastian up from the airport.

Walt went into Leo's gym to borrow his car. "How long are you working today?" Walt asked.

Leo handed Sebastian his keys. "I have a full day. I'll see you guys in the evening. We'll grab a few drinks with Sebastian."

Walt sipped on a bottle of Diet Coke. "Now you're talking my kind of language. I took the day off, so I could get a head start on the weekend. I'm going to be starting the party early."

Leo pulled up his schedule on his phone. "If you start drinking, make sure that Sebastian drives. Don't want you to drink and drive."

"I need to get out of here. I am allergic to gyms," said Walt.

Leo chuckled and shook his head.

"Bars and restaurants, I like." Walt waved and walked to the parking lot.

Walt drove to the airport and called Sebastian's phone. It went straight to voicemail.

Walt's phone rang, and he picked it up. "What's up, Sebastian?"

"Flight is delayed by a few hours man. Technical difficulties or something." Sebastian sounded irritated. "I fell asleep on the plane and just woke up. Plane hadn't moved."

Walt turned down the radio. "I know. I am at the airport. Should've checked the status before leaving. Anyway, I am going to park Leo's car in a lot and head to a bar. I'll text you the address of the parking lot and the bar. There are little lockers in the lot where I will leave the keys. You can pick up the keys and put your bags in the car. I will text you the code for the locker as well." Walt put on the turn signal and pulled onto the road.

"Don't get too hammered. I'll get the keys, put my bags in the car, and join you for a drink or two. See you soon" said Sebastian.

Walt heard a flight attendant tell Sebastian to turn off his cell phone.

"Later." Walt hung up the phone and drove to the parking lot. He parked and left the keys in the locker for Sebastian. He then got in a tuk tuk and headed to the bar.

Walt walked into the small dimly lit place and sat at the bar.

A young bartender with short blue hair and many visible tattoos approached Walt. "What can I get for you?"

Walt scanned the menu on his phone. "I have heard a lot about your margaritas and kati rolls. Let me start with one of each," said Walt. Kati rolls, a decadent and delicious street food comprising seasoned grilled meats and vegetables rolled inside wheat flatbreads was exactly what he needed.

"Good choice," said the tattooed bartender. She went into the kitchen and placed the order, after which she made the margarita.

Walt sipped on his first margarita when his phone rang. The caller ID on his phone showed his mother's number. "Hello, mother," he said, answering his phone with a huge smile. His mother's voice had a way of making him feel safe and happy.

"This is your father," said the voice on the other end of the phone.

Walt's smile turned to a frown when he heard the familiar voice of his father on the other line. "Why are you calling me from Ma's phone?" Walt asked.

The voice on the other end went shaky. "Your mother passed away. She is no more."

"What?" yelled Walt. "I spoke to her yesterday. How could this happen? How the hell could this happen?" Walt was paralyzed.

"The doctors are saying she had a brain aneurysm and died instantly." His father broke down. "There was nothing we could do to save her. Everything happened so suddenly."

Walt felt rage pulse through his body. His whole body trembled.

Walt's father sounded broken. "The reason I called is because I hope you can make it here sometime tomorrow. I plan to perform your mother's last rites the day after tomorrow. She would want you to be here." His father hung up the phone.

Walt was devastated. His support system had crashed. His mother was the one person in his family who understood him and supported him with everything he did. She was his rock, and now she wasn't going to be around. With the money from the heist, he was going to give his mother every comfort that money could buy, but she wouldn't be there to receive it. An uncontrollable grief came over him.

He went to the bathroom and locked himself in. He bawled. After he gained his composure, he reached into his pocket and grabbed a packet of ecstasy pills he took occasionally to get a feeling of euphoria. They stimulated oxytocin and reduced his feeling of misery. Instead of putting one pill into his mouth like he usually did, Walt popped two pills and went back to the bar to finish his margarita. The pills caused chemical reactions in his body, and he started feeling like he could take on the world. "Another margarita, please?" Walt's eyes glazed over.

"Coming right up," said the cheerful bartender.

Walt's phone rang. "The pilot gained some time, and we came in earlier than expected. My flight just landed, and I will be there shortly," said Sebastian.

"Sounds good, brother. I'll be right here at the bar." Walt's lip trembled.

"How much have you had to drink man? You are slurring," said Sebastian. Get a glass of water and order a drink for me.

"My mom is dead," said Walt. He fought back tears.

"Shit. I'm sorry man. I'll be there shortly." Walt hung up the phone.

The drugs had kicked in, and Walt slurred and was incoherent. Two burly men walked in and sat at the bar a few seats away from Walt. The men ordered drinks. One of the men nudged the other and pointed at Walt. Walt swayed on his bar stool with his eyes half closed while he hummed tunes. The two men made comments about Walt and snickered.

Walt got up from his bar stool and stumbled. "What the fuck are you pieces of trash looking at?"

One of the men who had numerous scars on his face stood up. "What the fuck did you say to me?" He advanced menacingly toward Walt.

The other man also got up from his seat.

"Fuck you," yelled Walt. He took his drink and threw it at the man with scars.

The enraged man hit Walt over the head with a bottle of beer. Walt crashed to the floor. He got up and grabbed a bottle of whiskey from the bar. "Do you know who I am? Do you?" He advanced toward the man with scars. "I am the guy who robbed the Royal Global Bank," Walt yelled.

The burly man with scars grabbed the bottle of whiskey and smashed it on Walt's head. Walt fell to the ground unconscious smashing his phone.

Two women stood by the bar and one of them pointed a gun at the man who hit Walt. "Freeze. You are under arrest."

The man with scars advanced toward her.

She fired a warning shot into the floor. "Get down on your knees and put your hands on your head, or the next bullet will go through you." The two men knelt and put their hands on their heads. "Grab a set of handcuffs from the jeep, Ava," the woman said.

Ava went to the jeep and came back with the cuffs.

"Secure them," said the woman.

Ava handcuffed both men.

Zubaria holstered her gun and picked up her phone. She made a call. "This is special agent Zubaria with Investigation Bureau. I need an ambulance right away. A man was hit on his head and is lying unconscious."

Ava checked Walt's vitals and found a pulse. She gave Zubaria the thumbs up.

Zubaria hung up and made another call. "Police station, this is special agent Zubaria. I need you to pick up two men and charge them with assault. I have handcuffed them, and they are waiting for you." She gave the person on the other end of the line the address to the bar.

She hung up and made a third call. "Hello, director, it's Zubaria. I picked up Ava from the airport and we headed to a hole in the wall place to grab lunch. You won't believe what happened here." She explained what happened. "The man lying unconscious on the floor claimed that he robbed the Royal Global Bank. I am getting him to a hospital, and once he regains consciousness, I will question him." She hung up the phone. Ambulance sirens approached.

Sebastian stood at the entrance of the bar looking shocked when he heard special agent Zubaria talking to the director of Investigation Bureau. He froze momentarily and then ran to Leo's car. He picked up his phone and made a call. "Leo, everything is over." He sounded frantic.

Leo went into an office in his gym and shut the door behind him. "What happened? Calm down, Sebastian. I can't understand what you are saying."

Sebastian told Leo what he had witnessed. "Walt was in a bad place. His mother died this morning."

Leo sank in his chair. He had a gut-wrenching feeling. It was only a matter of time before the cops got Walt to talk, and it would lead right back to all of them. He would be responsible for the destruction of not only his life, but also three others. "Sebastian, I need you to come and pick me up right now from the gym. I will call Isa and tell her what happened."

Sebastian hung up the phone and started the car with trembling hands.

Leo picked up his phone and dialed Isa's number. "Isa, I have some terrible news." Leo told Isa everything that had happened. "Sebastian and I are on our way to you." He hung up the phone.

Sebastian pulled Leo's car in front of the gym. "I guess this is karma catching up to us."

Leo punched the dashboard. He closed his eyes and meditated which calmed him down. "I hope Walt is okay. I can understand that in his terrible state of mind, he made a big mistake. Do you know what hospital they took him to?"

Sebastian gripped the steering wheel tight.

"We need to get to the hospital and figure out what state Walt is in," said Leo. "Once he wakes up, it won't take Investigation Bureau more than a couple of hours to break him and then get to us. Let's get Isa."

Sebastian drove the car and pulled into Isa's company.

Isa came to the car looking pale. "What's going to happen?" Isa got in the back seat and trembled.

"We have to go to the hospital where they are keeping Walt," said Leo.

Sebastian drove to the hospital where Walt was admitted.

"We need to get eyes inside the hospital," said Leo.

"Let me take a shot," said Sebastian. "I'll be back shortly." He walked into the front door of the hospital. He walked around and reached a room with the door ajar. He peeked his head in the room and found a doctor's coat hanging on a chair. He put on the coat and his glasses and walked out of the room.

Sebastian went to the reception desk. "Hello nurse there was a young man brought in today with a head injury. Which room is he in?" The numerous doctors and nurses in the hospital made it impossible to know who worked in the hospital and who didn't. Sebastian's lab coat gave him the perfect cover, and the nurse at the reception didn't ask him any questions.

"Let me check, doctor," said the nurse. She looked on her computer. "He is on the third floor in room three twenty-nine."

"Thank you, nurse." Sebastian took the stairs to the third floor. When he got close to Walt's room, he saw Zubaria in front on the room. She talked to two men in suits who stood guard outside Walt's room. The door to the room opened and a nurse came out with a clipboard. Sebastian followed the nurse. "Excuse me, nurse. How is the head trauma patient doing?" Sebastian asked.

"He is not in good shape, doctor. He is in a coma. The doctor on duty said that if he doesn't wake up in the next few days, it could be bad."

Sebastian thanked the nurse and headed back to the parking lot.

"How is he doing?" Isa asked.

Sebastian got in the passenger's seat. "He is in a coma. The nurse said that if he doesn't wake up in the next few days, his prognosis could be really bad."

Sebastian pointed animatedly at a woman who walked out of the hospital entrance. "She is the one who was at the bar. She brought Walt to the hospital and arrested the men who hit Walt."

Zubaria walked out of the hospital into the parking lot.

Leo watched Zubaria get in her jeep and drive away. "We need to know what is going on with Walt. There isn't a way to get close to him with two armed agents guarding the only access point to his room. How do we get eyes in the room?" Leo sighed.

"We can try and get a camera in the room," said Isa. Leo and Sebastian turned and looked at her.

"Nice," said Leo. "Let's do it."

Leo found a big box store on his phone and drove to it.

Sebastian went into the store and found a small battery-operated wireless camera. He also bought a burner smart phone. When he went to pay, his attention fell on a ceramic sculpture of an angel. Sebastian picked up the sculpture and a battery powered drill and paid for his items. He went back to the car and downloaded the camera app on the burner phone. He connected the camera to the phone. The phone screen showed images captured by the camera lens. Sebastian drilled a hole in the ceramic statue and hid the camera inside it. The lens pointed out of a hole in the sculpture. The phone showed video in the direction the sculpture faced. "I will go back in as the doctor and get the nurse to place it in Walt's room."

Leo drove back to the hospital.

Sebastian put on the lab coat and walked into the hospital. He connected the camera to the guest wireless network of the hospital. It worked great. He went to the third floor and stood by the coffee machine, a good vantage point, and he could see everyone who entered or exited Walt's room. He saw the nurse on duty come out of Walt's room and went up to her. "It's really sad that such a young person had to endure such violence. Can't believe he is in a coma." Sebastian shook his head.

The nurse pushed the button to call the elevator. "Yes, doctor, it is really sad."

Sebastian took out the sculpture of the angel from his lab coat. "Can you do me a favor? Even though our profession is based solely on science, I have seen some miracles happen in my lifetime. This sculpture has a lot of power. If you can place it by the patient's bedside facing him, I think it will help him and watch over him," said Sebastian. "I just used this on one of my patients, and it saved the little girl's life."

The nurse looked puzzled. She took the sculpture from Sebastian. "I am a superstitious person, doctor, but I have never met a doctor who is superstitious. If you think it will help him, I will do it right away." The nurse slipped the sculpture into her pocket walked back to Walt's room.

Sebastian came back to Leo's car. "We have eyes and ears in Walt's room." He showed Leo and Isa the burner phone. On the phone screen they saw Walt's motionless body lying on the bed. Machines beeped around him and he had tubes going in and out.

Isa's eyes welled up with tears.

"Let's go home and keep an eye on Walt," said Leo.

Whenever there was motion in Walt's room, the camera app on the phone chimed. The phone chimed late at night and Sebastian looked at the screen. He jumped out of his bed and called out to Leo.

Leo came out of his bedroom rubbing his eyes. "What's going on?" Leo asked.

"It's Walt. He has woken up." Sebastian showed Leo the phone. They saw Walt look left and right not knowing where he was. The two agents who stood guard appeared on the screen. The nurse on duty appeared on the screen.

"He's awake. Now what? It's only a matter of time," Leo said as his mind raced. The nurse injected something into Walt's intravenous line, and he calmed down.

Special agent Zubaria walked into Walt's room shortly and pulled up a chair beside his bed. She handed Walt a glass of water, which he gulped down. "Alcohol, drugs, and getting clobbered in the head are not a good combination," said Zubaria. "How are you feeling?"

She held up Walt's wallet and pulled out his driver's license. "It's good to meet you."

Walt stared at her blankly. He then uttered his first words. "Who am I? Where am I? I can't remember anything."

"Ah, amnesia," said Zubaria. "Do you not remember anything?" She crossed her left leg over her right and leaned back in her chair.

"I have a strange feeling in my head and I can't remember anything." Walt looked around the room.

"Well, the reason I am here is that before you got hit on the head, you confessed to robbing the Royal Global Bank." Zubaria leaned closer to Walt.

Walt stared at her without showing any emotion.

She looked carefully at Walt. "I am sorry that you don't remember anything. I will come and visit you once the doctors have examined you."

Zubaria got up from her chair and walked to the door. She turned around. "We just got news that your mother was murdered by your father, and he has been arrested."

"My mother died of a brain aneurysm," yelled Walt.

Zubaria smiled.

CHAPTER THIRTEEN

DEVIL'S ROCK

Mumbai, August 2018

A prison nicknamed Devil's Rock stood on an island one mile off the coast of Mumbai. It used to be a weapons manufacturing facility built by the British in the late 1800s. When the facility was in operation, it earned the nickname The Death Factory. After India gained independence from the British in 1947, the facility lay vacant for many years until the government decided to make it a prison in the late 1990s. The concrete plus-sign-shaped building stood eighty feet high. A thick fifty-foot-high brick wall surrounded the whole prison. Five feet of electrified fencing on top of the wall ensured that anyone who tried to scale the wall would be fried. The wrought iron front gate featured the royal coat of arms of the United Kingdom, a shield with a golden lion on one side and a silver unicorn on the other. The government had decided to keep the symbol because it was a beautiful work of art, even though it represented the royalty of the United Kingdom. Perched on top of the wall on either side of the gate were dragons with eyes red as embers of coal that breathed fire. The menacing dragons were visible from the shore. Lights from the ground illuminated the dragons and made them look ethereal. At night the bright lights inside the dragon's eyes were switched on, making them visible from shore on a clear night.

The prison system prided itself on the fact that no prisoner had escaped Devil's Rock. Most of the funding came from the government, because officials were happy to keep the dangerous inmates of Devil's Rock isolated from the civilian population. Devil's Rock had ties to pharmaceutical companies that tested new drugs and medical procedures on inmates that volunteered. The inmates who signed waivers and agreed to be guinea pigs for the pharmaceutical companies received special perks, such as radios in their cells, access to cigarettes, and in some cases access to alcohol. Most of the vegetables that fed the inmates were grown on the premises. A group of inmates managed the chicken coops and supplied meat and eggs. Even the milk that was used in the prison came from cows tended by a group of inmates. The warden took pride in the fact that Devil's Rock had built a sustainable system.

Across from the islands, an old ferry with the name Prison Queen painted on its side was moored at an old pier. Men in handcuffs stood in a line and waited their turn to get onto the ferry.

A toothless older man grinned. "Welcome aboard, please take a seat wherever you want. We hope you have a wonderful experience aboard our boat."

Another man wearing overalls snickered.

Leo walked onto the boat with his hands cuffed in front of him. Six other men with their hands cuffed followed Leo onto the boat.

Four policemen jumped aboard and took their seats on the boat.

"That's all of our inmates. Let's get this over with," one of the policemen said.

The old toothless man closed the gate and removed the rope that secured the boat to land. "We welcome you and hope you enjoy your journey with us."

One of the policemen shook his head.

Another policeman snickered.

The ferry roared as it moved forward. A short and choppy ride later, the ferry stopped. Six uniformed guards came aboard the ferry. One of the guards exchanged paperwork with the policemen while the others made the prisoners stand on the dock in a single file.

A feeling of gloom came over Leo when he imagined his life in a maximum-security prison. His thoughts were interrupted by one of the prison guards.

"Gentlemen, please walk in a single file to the gate," the lead prison guard said.

The prison building loomed, looking ominous with its huge walls and fire-breathing dragons. The ethereal appeal and the architectural beauty mesmerized Leo. He thought of Isa and how she would've loved the architecture of this place.

A small portal opened on the giant wrought-iron gate. The prisoners entered the portal maintaining a single file. Leo was pleasantly surprised at how green the landscape was. There was a beautiful lawn with trees and flowering plants scattered around it. "Wow! Not what I was expecting," said Leo out loud to himself.

A man wearing a button-down shirt and khaki pants stepped forward. "Impressive, isn't it? Welcome to Devil's Rock. I am the warden, and I have three simple rules. Stay out of trouble, contribute to Devil's Rock, and use your time here as an opportunity to reform yourself." He paced back and forth and made eye contact with each of the prisoners. "The guards will search you and escort you to your cells." The warden signaled the head security guard.

The inmates were taken to a large room where their handcuffs were removed. They were made to undress and searched thoroughly. The guards hosed them down with cold water and gave them towels and their prison uniforms. "Get changed, and you will be taken to your cells."

Leo dried off and put on his blue jumpsuit, the only outfit he would get to wear for a long time.

Two guards escorted Leo to his cell. "Fresh meat," yelled some of the prisoners as Leo passed their cells. One thing Leo knew about prisons was that if he showed fear, it would be his end. His years of mixed martial arts training were going to come in handy to save his life.

One of the guards opened the cell, while the other uncuffed Leo. "Stay out of trouble, and you will be okay, boy," said one of the guards. "If you mess up, we won't show you any mercy. Your cellmate is a newbie just like you. You guys have so much in common, maybe you can be lovers." Both the guards snickered. The guard locked the cell.

Leo looked around the cell and estimated it to be about twelve feet wide and long. There was a steel toilet and sink in one corner. Half the space in the cell was taken up by bunk beds. There was a small window in the cell through which he could see the twilight sky.

A large man slept on the top bunk. Leo lay on the bottom bunk and stared at the bottom of the top bunk. The feeling of having a door right in front of him but not being able to open it hit Leo suddenly. This was what not having freedom felt like. He thought about Isa and her beautiful face, and it calmed him down. He was exhausted and fell asleep right away.

When he woke up, his cellmate sat on the floor and stared at him. His cellmate was six feet two inches and heavily built. He had a bald head and a thick moustache.

Leo jumped out of his bed. "What the hell are you staring at?"

"Relax," said the big man. "I was just reading my novel." He held up the novel he was reading.

"Sorry, I didn't mean any disrespect," said Leo. "I'm Leo." Leo extended his hand.

"They call me Arnold," said the big man, shaking Leo's hand. Arnold was a big man, but his voice was soft and calm.

"What brought you to this paradise?" asked Leo.

"A man tried to hurt my wife and daughter, and I confronted him." Arnold put his novel down. "Things got out of hand, and I killed him." He didn't flinch. "You have nothing to fear, Leo. I am just here to do my time and get back to my family." He pulled out a photo of his wife and daughter from inside his novel and showed it to Leo.

As time went by, Leo got into a routine. The cell doors were opened at six a.m. and the inmates needed to get back to their cells by six p.m. Food was served in the middle section of the building, and inmates from all blocks got to meet each other. The prison was filled with murderers, rapists, drug dealers, human traffickers, pedophiles, and all other kinds of criminals.

Gradually Leo found out that gangs operated within the premises of Devil's Rock. High-profile criminals who inhabited Devil's Rock ran its gangs.

Leo usually ate lunch with Arnold, but Arnold was called into work one afternoon, so Leo was having lunch alone. Three inmates who sat at a different table went to Leo's table and stood in front of it. The inmate in the middle seemed to be the leader and the other two seemed to be lackeys. The man in the middle sat down across from Leo. The lackeys sat on either side of the leader.

The inmate in the middle put his arms on the table displaying numerous tattoos of black roses. "Each of the roses represents one of my bitches."

The lackeys grinned. The man in the middle smacked his lips and winked at Leo.

Leo felt pangs of fear but remained composed.

"After lunch, come over to his cell and he will make you feel good," said one of the lackeys. "If you don't, we will end you."

The other lackey pulled a shank from his jumpsuit and placed it on the table.

Prisoners at nearby tables were eyeing the encounter, some with sympathy and others with disinterest. Leo got up and grabbed one of the lackey's arms and slammed it on the table, elbow facing up. He jammed a foot down on his elbow with a cracking noise, and the lackey fell to the floor clutching his broken arm and letting out a high-pitched scream. The second lackey lunged at Leo with his shank. Leo threw a roundhouse kick, catching him square in the jaw. The second lackey collapsed and didn't move. The leader came at Leo. Leo subdued him, held his head down with his mouth against the edge of the table, and crashed a knee on the back of the man's head. The man hit the floor screaming in agony as blood oozed out of his mouth and several of his teeth fell out.

Leo stood up tall and looked around the room with the most intense stare he could muster. His message to everyone was, if you mess with me, I will fuck you up. He felt a sharp pain in his back and collapsed. One of the security guards had incapacitated Leo with a taser. When Leo woke up, he was in a dark, confined space. "Where am I?" Leo yelled banging on the walls.

There was a loud thud as a guard hit the box with a baton. "Welcome to solitary confinement, boy," the guard yelled. "Enjoy the next twenty-four hours here."

Twenty-four hours seemed like an eternity as Leo struggled to keep his sanity. The door opened, and he was relieved to see a guard. "Back to your cell, inmate," said the guard, brandishing his baton. "This is your first and last warning. Next time, your sentence will be increased."

The guard let Leo into his cell.

Arnold shook his head. "The one day I am not with you and you get into trouble. What were you thinking beating the shit out of three guys?"

Leo lay on his bed. "Those pieces of trash had it coming. It seemed like a good idea at the time." He fluffed his pillow. "I never thought I would say this, but I missed this cell."

Arnold chuckled. "You are lucky they didn't increase your sentence. Better keep a low profile from now on."

Weeks passed, and Leo found that his cafeteria stunt had given other inmates the right message. No one tried to mess with him, which was a relief. The fact that Arnold was with him kept him safe. Arnold was a big dude and intimidated most people.

Arnold and Leo were sitting in the garden one afternoon. All the other inmates got up abruptly and left the garden. Not too far from where Leo and Arnold sat, an older man slept on the grass. Three men guarded the sleeping man.

Suddenly five men with their faces covered and holding shanks ran across the lawn toward the sleeping man. As the masked men got close, the bodyguards fought them off. The masked men outnumbered the bodyguards, and two of them had gotten free. As the free masked men advanced toward the sleeping man, Leo and Arnold charged toward them. One of the masked men had raised his shank and was about to sink it into the sleeping man's chest when Leo grabbed him by the neck and saved the sleeping man.

The sleeping man woke up and watched his men fighting the masked assailants. The assailants took off while the bodyguards told the sleeping man they had been ambushed.

The older man approached Leo and Arnold. "Thank you for saving my life." He shook Leo and Arnold's hands. "Get out of here before the guards come or we will be in trouble." The man left with his bodyguards. Leo and Arnold walked out of the garden quietly. They hurried back to their cell.

The next day at lunch, a man came up to Leo and Arnold. "Stalin would like to invite you to join him for lunch." He pointed to a table where the man they saved sat with a group of people.

Leo and Arnold got up and followed the man to Stalin's table.

Stalin pointed to two empty seats. "Welcome to my table. Please have a seat. I am Stalin Mahadevan. Stalin. I am the leader of the one of the five gangs and want to thank you for saving my life. He extended his hand.

Leo and Arnold shook his hand.

"I am Leo, and this is Arnold," said Leo.

Stalin was in his early fifties and had graying hair. He was about five feet seven and well built. "Stalin can't be killed that easily," said Stalin, putting his right hand across his chest.

"Do you know who attacked you yesterday?" Leo asked.

"Not yet. The faces of the assailants were covered, and we couldn't tell which gang they were associated with. All the gangs have an agreement not to harm members of other gangs and not to interfere in their operations. It is surprising that someone tried to take me out, because it would cause unnecessary bloodshed and loss."

Leo noticed inmates sitting at other tables eyeing Stalin's table.

"Don't worry," said Stalin. "People are intrigued to see who the new recruits in Stalin's gang are. We don't recruit just anyone, only the best."

Leo paused before responding. "With all due respect, Stalin, I am not looking for any trouble and am just trying to do my time and get out," said Leo calmly.

Stalin scratched his beard. "Understandable. This place is filled with violent criminals and when they know that someone is close to getting out, they either find a way to stop someone from getting out or make sure they get out in a body bag. If people think that you are affiliated with my organization, it will guarantee you a certain level of protection and make you untouchable."

Says the guy who almost got killed yesterday, Leo thought.

Stalin squinted. "This is the first time someone has gotten that close to killing me in prison. They will be found and made an example of. No one else will dare to think about harming Stalin." He seemed to read Leo's thoughts. "That's enough for today," said Stalin. "I owe you both for saving my life and would like to repay the debt." Stalin got up from the table and walked away with his men.

The next time Leo saw Stalin was four days later. "How is prison life?" Stalin asked. "Any trouble?"

"Not at all," said Leo. "Arnold and I have been transferred from laundry services to the kitchen. It happened suddenly."

Stalin chuckled. "You will be among friends in the kitchen."

Leo was puzzled. "Did you have us transferred?"

"I did. Everyone who works in the kitchen is in my gang." Stalin ate a mouthful of food and looked at Leo. "Is that okay with you?"

"Thank you." Leo headed back to his cell after lunch.

Weeks passed, and Leo's interactions with Stalin increased. Leo sat with Stalin in the garden one afternoon. "How did you end up here, Stalin, and how long are you in for?" Leo asked.

Stalin placed his arm on Leo's shoulder. "Do you want to hear the story of how Stalin Mahadevan, the skinny and studious boy, became Stalin the notorious gangster?"

"I do," said Leo.

Stalin cleared his throat. "I grew up in a small village on the outskirts of Chennai. My mother was a teacher, and my father a journalist. On my tenth birthday, my life was turned upside down. My father published a story exposing a local mobster. The mobster was arrested but released for lack of evidence and was out for blood. On my tenth birthday, my parents were celebrating my birthday in our little house. Just as we were going to cut my birthday cake, there was a knock on the door. When my father opened the door, the mobster and a few of his goons barged in and knocked my father down. My father and I were tied to chairs and made to sit facing the bed. We were forced to watch my mother being raped by the mobster and his goons repeatedly. They then stabbed her until she was dead. The cloth tied around my father's and my mouth muffled our screams. The goons threw my father on the floor, and the mobster bludgeoned him to death with an iron rod. I went into shock. The mobster told one of his men to untie me and said they were going to celebrate my birthday. They made me blow out the candles on my cake while they sang happy birthday. They made me cut the cake and eat a piece before the mobster took the iron rod to my legs and broke both my shins. The mobster told his goons to lock the door from the outside and set the house on fire. They locked me inside and set fire to the house. I crawled out of a small window at the back of the house. It took all my strength, but I got the window open and climbed through it into the backyard. I heard a loud explosion, and the whole house went up in flames." Stalin sighed deeply.

Leo gulped. "I am sorry Stalin. I can't imagine experiencing the kind of pain and suffering that you did."

Stalin stroked his beard. His eyes were bloodshot. "It was a long time ago," he said. "The humanity in me died that day," said Stalin.

"What happened to the mobster?" Leo asked.

Stalin laughed maniacally. "My neighbors found me and took care of me until my legs healed. After that, I was on the street learning to fend for myself. I went to multiple juvenile homes for petty crimes over the next few years. It was a juvenile home where I met my mentor and partner, Musa. Musa was part of a gang that was always on the lookout for promising talent to recruit. The gang Musa was a part of was involved in drug and human trafficking. I spent six years training with Musa's gang and grew in their ranks. Musa came to me one day and told me that he had found the mobster who had killed my parents. As you can imagine, this was music to my ears. Musa and I took about thirty people and headed to the town where the mobster lived in a heavily guarded mansion outside the village and now had a family. He was married with two kids. I went to his house and recreated the scene from my tenth birthday, but it was more brutal. Once my people raped his wife and slit her throat, they killed his children. After he watched his family die, I broke most of the bones in his body using a sledgehammer. I burned down his house and made sure that no one survived." Stalin looked at Leo to see his reaction.

A chill went down Leo's spine. He kept his poker face. "The son of a bitch got what he deserved."

It seemed to be the perfect response because Stalin smiled and patted Leo on his shoulders. "That was how Stalin was born. Musa and I built an empire from that point forward," said Stalin proudly.

"How did you end up here?" Leo asked.

Stalin stretched. "Fate has a funny way of changing the course of people's lives. I was in London meeting with a potential customer who would also distribute drugs for me. After closing the deal, we had a few drinks, and I was driving back to my hotel room. My car was hit by another car that had run a red light. There was a police car in the vicinity, and it reached the crash site right away. I was arrested for driving under the influence of alcohol and taken into custody by British authorities. They collected my fingerprints and sent them to Indian authorities. I was extradited back to India and ended up here. I am here because some jackass ran a red light and rammed into my Maserati."

Leo shook his head.

Stalin stood up. "That's all for today. I got some business to take care of." He walked away.

Leo let out a deep sigh. Stalin was a monster that had been created because of the brutal circumstances in his life. He was a monster nevertheless.

***

Stalin ate lunch with Leo one afternoon. "Leo, I am going to do you a favor."

Leo looked puzzled. "A favor? What is it?"

Stalin chewed on his food. "I am going to pull some strings and get you a job waiting tables at Devil's Rock restaurant and bar."

Leo stopped eating. "Haven't heard of that place."

Devil's Rock restaurant and bar was the brainchild of the warden. It was a lucrative endeavor for Devil's Rock. One Saturday night every month, the staff converted a small section of the courtyard into a restaurant and bar. Civilians bought tickets to wine and dine there. Included as part of the package was a boat tour showcasing the history of Devil's Rock. The boat tour also introduced the high-profile criminals who were inmates at Devil's Rock. The visitors got a chance to explore the green courtyard and have a three-course meal prepared and served by the inmates. Inmates who worked at Devil's Rock restaurant and bar wore electric collars controlled by guards who would incapacitate inmates who were out of line.

"You can ask your friends to buy the dinner package, and you will be able to see them. That's the only way inmates ever get to visit friends or family," said Stalin.

Leo's eyes lit up. "You would do that for me?"

"Of course," said Stalin. "You saved my life. It's the least I can do. It makes the sentence easier."

Leo grinned. "Thank you, Stalin. This is the best news I have heard in a while."

"Absolutely," said Stalin. "You have a lot of potential. Besides, when the time comes, you can do me a favor."

Sometimes you need to dance with the devil, thought Leo. He shook Stalin's hand with both his hands.

Leo walked towards his cell feeling ecstatic, when he saw a familiar face. He went up to the man. "Sinha?"

The man jumped while letting out a loud yelp. "Please don't do anything to me." Sinha cowered and placed his back against the wall.

"You are in the right place," said Leo.

Sinha, the man who had raped Isa, looked broken and scared. He shivered and hobbled away with his head held down.

An older blind man who had been with Sinha stayed behind. Leo asked what happened to Sinha.

"News had leaked that Sinha was a pedophile," said the old blind man. "We may be criminals, but we don't take kindly to pedophiles.

Sinha gets beaten up and sodomised on a regular basis," the old man said. "He won't survive long. If someone doesn't kill him, he will take his own life."

Leo didn't feel sorry for Sinha. He deserved what he got.

***

On the day that Isa, Sebastian, and Walt were going to visit, Leo couldn't contain his excitement. He would meet the people closest in his life.

That evening, Leo trimmed his beard, and put on his waiter's uniform. He headed to the cafeteria.

The head prison guard came into the cafeteria. "Dinner guests will be arriving in an hour." Leo's heart raced, and he grinned.

"What are you grinning about inmate?" The guard asked.

"Oh, nothing sir," said Leo. "I am just happy to meet someone who is not from the prison."

"If you try any funny business, you will be shocked with electricity, and that is not pleasant," said the guard.

The guard slipped on the electric collar around Leo's neck. There were three waiters including Leo, and each was going to manage five tables.

The guards took the waiters out to the courtyard where the restaurant tables were setup. There were three sections of five tables each, and Leo stood by the tables in his section. He stared at the entrance door eagerly.

Devil's Rock bar and restaurant was marketed as a fine dining establishment and it charged a steep fee for what it called Devil's Rock experience.

The door opened. An older couple dressed formally came into the restaurant. They sat down at the table nearest to the entrance. Next, three middle-aged women in revealing clothes walked in. They scoped out the restaurant and went to one of Leo's tables. The sight of the scantily clad women started to awaken his desire. His carnal thoughts were interrupted by the next group that came in to the restaurant. It was a group of fifteen people, and they went to Leo's area. Leo combined three tables to accommodate the whole group. There was only one table left in Leo's section.

A few other groups of people came in and seated themselves. Leo saw Isa, Walt, and Sebastian come through the door and he motioned for them to sit at his last table. They walked over to Leo's area quickly. A huge grin came over Leo's face as he pulled a chair out for Isa. Isa was wearing a blue evening gown that accentuated her figure. Leo couldn't take his eyes off her. Isa grabbed Leo and kissed him on the lips causing one of the guards to step forward.

Leo felt warm and didn't want to let Isa go. "No touching the inmates," said the guard. "Next time I will shock him with electricity."

"Sorry." Isa waved to the guard. "How are you, Leo? I miss you." Isa's eyes welled up.

Leo smiled. "I am okay. I even made friends here. How are you guys doing?"

Sebastian and Walt hugged Leo.

The guard threw his arms up in the air.

Walt mouthed the words sorry to the guard.

Isa sat down." You look handsome with the beard and long hair."

Leo touched his beard. "You look beautiful, Isa," said Leo. "Seeing you walk in the door took my breath away, just like the first time I saw you."

Isa blushed.

One of the men from the large group stood up. "Waiter! You have other tables here as well."

Leo went over to the large table and took their drink orders. Next, he went to the table where the three women sat. "What can I start you ladies off with?" Leo asked.

One of the women bit her lip. "I could eat you up." The women derived sadistic pleasure from flirting with Leo and trying to turn him on.

Another woman reached out and grabbed Leo's crotch. "I would like that."

The women giggled when they saw Leo's reaction.

Leo felt a fire inside him, and his crotch started to swell. He went to the kitchen abruptly and cooled off inside the meat cooler to avoid an embarrassing situation. A few moments in the cooler calmed him down.

The group of fifteen people left at the end of the dinner and dessert. The table with the three women left him a handsome tip. They also left him their email addresses on a napkin. "We would love to send you pictures and videos. Come find us when you get out of prison. We share everything." The women blew kisses at Leo and left.

Isa kissed Leo hungrily on his lips and Leo kissed her back. It earned Leo a zap. "It was worth it," said Leo with a smile.

"I love you," said Isa as she was escorted out by the guards.

Leo was shepherded back to his cell a happy man. He fell asleep with a smile on his face. He had an epiphany in the early hours of dawn. His first day of working at Devil's Rock restaurant and bar had given him an idea. He couldn't wait to meet and tell Stalin his idea.

Stalin spent a few hours in the greenhouse every morning, his equivalent of therapy, which gave him solace. Leo went to the greenhouse and found Stalin's bodyguards outside. "I need to talk to Stalin urgently. I know this is his time of solitude, but I think he will want to hear what I have to say."

One of the bodyguards went inside. He came out and signaled for Leo to go inside.

Stalin trimmed a shrub while humming a tune. The once-notorious mobster and murderer was now caged like an animal and took care of plants. "Have a seat. What's on your mind?" He continued to trim the shrub.

"Stalin, I have a plan," said Leo.

"A plan for what?" Stalin hummed his tune.

"I want to break you out of Devil's Rock." Leo took a few steps closer to Stalin.

Stalin stopped and turned to face Leo. "Leo, my partner, Musa, has sent many people on boats to try to break me out of here. The one thing they don't tell you is that this place has a miniature army of its own. They have anti-aircraft machine guns all around Devil's Rock. Once the boats that came to rescue me were in firing range, the guards lit the boats up. The skeletons of the people that Musa had hired to rescue me are at the bottom of the ocean. Well, bits and pieces of their skeletons." Stalin placed his hand on Leo's shoulder. "This place is a fortress. It's impossible to break out of here." Stalin went back to trimming the shrub.

"What I hear you say is that it is impossible to break someone out of here using force," said Leo. "I am talking about using the technique of deception. I will be released soon, and I will break you out."

Stalin put his tools down and walked toward Leo. "Why would you risk your life for me once you get out?"

"Once I get out of here, I will be labeled a felon and won't be able to find respect or a job in society," said Leo. "I would like to be a part of your business." Leo saw hope in Stalin's eyes.

"What is your plan?" Stalin grabbed a chair for Leo. Leo sat on the chair and Stalin pulled up another chair beside him.

Leo sat at the edge of his chair. "The only way guards will voluntarily take you off Devil's Rock is if you are so sick that you cannot be treated here."

Stalin's eyes opened wide. "How will I get so sick that the doctors here won't be able to diagnose me?"

"Leave that to me," said Leo. "I have a friend on the outside who is a whiz with chemicals, and I will have him whip up a concoction that will get you very sick. The doctors here will have to take you to a hospital on land."

Stalin rubbed his palms together. "Never thought about that. How will you get the chemical to me?"

"Devil's Rock bar and restaurant. We will have one of your people bring it in and give it to a waiter in the restaurant. Once it gets in the hands of the waiter, it will find its way to you."

Stalin's eyes opened wide. "Genius." Stalin got up from the chair and paced the greenhouse. "You may pull off the impossible after all. You will be a great addition to my business, and you will be rich beyond your dreams. You can buy respect." Stalin clapped loudly. "I knew you were special the first time I met you."

"Thank you. Let me work the details out. I am being released in a few weeks." Leo walked out of the greenhouse feeling enthusiastic.

***

The day before Leo's release, he had lunch with Stalin.

Stalin was in a great mood. "Take this letter. The address listed in the letter is in a small village outside of Nilambur forests, a dense forest range in the state of Kerala. Find the Forest Restaurant and tell the owner you are looking for the Gateway to Hell. Musa will find you, and when he does, give him my letter. He will take care of the rest. I hope to see you on the other side." Stalin stood up and hugged Leo.

"Arnold is getting released in a few weeks on probation. Are you okay with me taking Arnold to see Musa? Arnold is like a brother to me," Leo said.

"Of course, I owe Arnold as much as I owe you. Both of you saved my life. Together we will make my empire greater." Stalin had a spring in his step when he walked away.

The guards came to Leo's cell early the next morning. "Time to go, inmate," one of the guards said.

"I will see you in a few weeks," Leo told his cellmate.

Arnold nodded but didn't say a word, in typical Arnold style.

The warden waited for Leo at the courtyard. "Every time an inmate is released, which isn't often, my tradition is to walk him to the boat that will take him to his freedom. I also give him the money he has earned and extra money to buy his first meal on the outside. You are only the third person to get released in all my years of being warden on Devil's Rock." The warden put his arm on Leo's shoulder and walked him out.

The guards opened the portal on the large gate, and Leo got his first glimpse of the Mumbai skyline. He stared at the skyline for a few moments, enjoying his freedom. He breathed in the cool ocean air.

"Thank you, warden. I wasn't sure I would survive in here for a year. Freedom feels incredible, and I won't take it for granted ever again."

Leo extended his hand to the warden.

"Be good. I wish you the best." The warden shook Leo's hand firmly and bid him farewell.

Leo got onto the boat that would take him to his freedom. The cool ocean breeze hit his face as the boat started through the choppy water.

The Prison Queen pulled up at the harbor. Leo stepped out and bid the men on the boat farewell.

CHAPTER FOURTEEN

THE GREAT ESCAPE

Mumbai, August 2019

Arnold was released from Devil's Rock a few weeks after Leo. He went home and spent time with his wife and daughter. Arnold then took a train to Mumbai and called Leo. Leo and Arnold would make the journey to the forest village the next morning, where they would meet Stalin's partner.

Arnold and Leo met at the airport a couple of hours before their flight the next morning. Leo carried the letter that Stalin had given him. There was a high probability of Leo and Arnold disappearing if they went to meet Musa without Stalin's letter.

They hopped on a flight from Mumbai to Kochi, Kerala. The forest village was about 150 miles from Kochi airport. Leo and Arnold got into a cab from Kochi airport and took the journey to the village. The cab rode over meandering roads with picturesque scenery before reaching the village. Leo paid the cab driver, and he drove away.

Look looked around. "Did you notice how people went into their houses and closed their doors when our cab pulled up? We are in a ghost town suddenly," he said.

"There is a little shop," said Arnold, pointing to the only place with its doors open.

Leo and Arnold walked in the direction of the little shop. Leo walked in through the open door. "We are looking for the Forest Restaurant. Can you tell us where it is?" Leo asked in Malayalam, the native tongue of Kerala.

A toothless old woman hobbled toward Leo and Arnold. She flashed them a toothless grin. "You are in the right place. We need to repaint the sign." The woman pointed to a faded sign on the wall that was barely visible. Before Leo could ask his next question, she spoke. "Sit down, and I will get you our specialty dish of the day." She hobbled into another room through a small door.

Leo as he sat on a bench. "Malayalam is the longest palindrome I know," he said.

Arnold stared at him blankly.

Leo explained to Arnold what a palindrome was.

The old woman came out with two cups of piping hot tea and placed them on the table. "Drink it." She smiled.

Leo took a sip of the tea and smacked his lips. "This is the best tea I have had in my life. The flavors of cardamom and ginger elevate the taste of the tea."

Arnold gave the old woman a thumbs up. Malayalam wasn't one of the languages Arnold spoke.

The woman sat down at another table. "Farmers from our village grow the cardamom and ginger. What do big city people call it? Ah yes, organic. Everything grown by our farmers is organic. That is the secret of our tea." She winked at Leo.

Leo chuckled. The old woman could've been in sales or marketing.

"We are looking for the gateway to hell," said Leo.

As soon as he said those words, a man who sat in a corner of the restaurant got up. As he walked out of the restaurant, he gestured for Leo and Arnold to wait.

The old woman brought in two plates of piping hot plantain fritters. "This is our special of the day." She placed the two plates on the table. "Try it."

Leo's eyes grew wide with excitement. "I haven't eaten plantain fritters in a long time." Leo rubbed his palms together. "Can we get two more glasses of tea, please?" Leo asked the old woman. Leo took the first bite and closed his eyes. "Incredible. Much tastier than I remember."

The old woman chuckled. She went in to the room and came back with two more glasses of tea.

Arnold finished both fritters in less than a minute. He smacked his lips. "Delicious," he said.

"He will need one more plate," said Leo with a chuckle.

The old woman yelled at someone inside, asking him to bring out two more plates.

Two men who wore black came into the restaurant. Both men had handguns holstered on one hip and machetes on the other. The men also had rifles slung on their shoulders. "Why do you want to find the gateway to hell?" one of the men asked Leo.

"We were sent by Stalin to find Musa," said Leo. "I have a letter from Stalin."

Both men jumped when they heard Stalin's name. One of the men took off running.

Leo thanked the old woman and paid her much more than what he owed. The woman's eyes lit up.

The man who took off running came back in panting and whispered something in the other man's ear.

"Let's go." One of the men said to Leo and Arnold.

Leo and Arnold waved to the old woman and followed the two men out of the restaurant.

The sunset with the picturesque sky as the background took Leo's breath away. He pulled out his cellphone and clicked pictures of the mesmerizing collage of colors. "This place is breathtaking. A very different kind of beauty compared to that of Mumbai."

The men paused and let Leo take in the view.

"Let's go," said one of the men.

Leo and Arnold followed the two men.

The men took small flashlights out of their pockets and turned them on. They had reached the outskirts of the woods, and once they entered the tree canopy, it would be dark. A short walk later, the two men turned to face Leo and Arnold.

The forest thicket was dense. The men had to speak loudly to be heard over the noises made by insects that inhabited the forest ecosystem. The men took their rifles off their shoulders and pointed them at Leo and Arnold. Leo and Arnold put their hands up and stepped back. The two men cackled when they saw the look of fear on Leo and Arnold's faces.

A deep voice came from behind a large tree. "If you fools are done screwing around, can I have a conversation with these people?" The silhouette of a man got closer to the two men holding the guns. The man hobbled and used a walking stick with a serpent's head on top. The eyes of the serpent glowed green. The man stopped. "I am Musa, and I heard that you are looking for the gateway to hell. Who are you?" The man stepped closer to Leo and Arnold. He was older and had gray hair and a graying moustache and beard.

Leo stepped forward. "I am Leo, and this is Arnold. We were sent by Stalin. We were on Devil's Rock together." Leo took the letter from his backpack and handed it to Musa. "Stalin wanted us to give this to you."

Musa grabbed the letter from Leo's hand. He took a few steps away and turned his back to Leo and Arnold. He switched on a flashlight and read the letter. He then looked at Leo and Arnold with a huge grin. "Welcome to Netherworld, our organization. We have a lot to talk about. Follow me." He hobbled toward a large tree.

Leo and Arnold followed Musa, and the armed men walked behind them.

Musa pulled out a remote and pushed a button as soon as passed a large tree. There was a mechanical sound as the land in front moved. "Welcome to the gateway to hell." Musa beamed.

The armed men pulled on handles that opened a heavy wrought iron lid. There was a large hole in the ground underneath. A stairway led down the hole in the ground. The outside of the lid was lined with shrubs and plants to camouflage it and make it blend in with the surroundings. Musa walked down the stairway, and Leo and Arnold followed. Once they were down the stairs, Musa pulled out his remote and pushed a button. The lid closed with a mechanical noise. One of the armed men secured the lid from the inside.

"What do you think?" Musa asked with excitement.

"My mind is blown," said Leo. "Incredible setup. Wouldn't have guessed this place existed."

"That is the point," said Musa. A large scar ran all the way from Musa's left cheek to his Adam's apple.

Leo tried not to stare, but Musa had already noticed Leo looking at the scar. "A tiger mauled me many years ago. I ripped its heart out and made a rug from its skin." Musa laughed maniacally.

Leo felt a chill run down his spine. Musa and Stalin were similar.

The men stood at the end of a dimly lit tunnel near a jeep. One of the armed men got in the driver's seat. Musa got in front and told Leo and Arnold to sit in the back. The second armed man got in the back with Leo and Arnold. After a short ride, the jeep stopped in a much larger space.

Musa smiled at seeing the admiration on Leo's and Arnold's faces. "What do you think of our setup?" Musa got out of the jeep.

"Wow," said Leo. "How does a place like this get power without being on the grid? I assume you are not on the grid. If you were, people would know this place existed."

"Smart question. I understand what Stalin sees in you," said Musa. "We employed the best engineers to build a setup that generates hydroelectricity from the river that runs above us."

"Brilliant. I guess you can get internet connectivity without causing too much suspicion," asked Leo.

"Absolutely," said Musa.

"I want to show you where this tunnel leads before showing you the main area." The jeep drove into a bigger tunnel for about ten minutes before it reached a large space that smelled damp. "Come with me." Musa got out of the jeep and motioned for Leo and Arnold to follow. Leo heard running water and realized that they were at the river. He followed Musa and reached a staircase. Musa walked down the stairs, and Leo and Arnold followed.

"Impressive setup," said Arnold.

Musa pointed to three large boats that were docked. "Two of the boats transport our drugs, and the other one handles our flesh trade." Musa had a menacing grin. "All boats have secret compartments, and nothing is found when we are searched. The entrance to the river is blocked using rocks that move at will for boats to enter or exit. From the outside, no one will ever be able to tell that such a place exists. All they see are the large rocks on the banks of the river. The river connects to the ocean and takes our supply chain to the next level. We can efficiently supply goods to our distributors and customers." Musa's chest swelled with pride.

"Musa, I have never seen anything like it," said Leo.

"Stalin and I built this together." Musa beamed. "It took us about ten years to get it fully operational. Let's go to the main area." Musa walked back up the staircase.

The jeep drove them back to the large space. Muse got off the jeep and walked into a room the size of a tennis court. "This is our packaging facility." The room had dozens of large tables with neatly wrapped packages sitting on them.

They next stopped at a large temperature-controlled greenhouse. "This is where the magic happens. We grow coca plants here that are used to make cocaine. We also grow cannabis plants for marijuana. We employed scientists to help manufacture top-quality products. We can make about eighty pounds of cocaine every eighteen months and five hundred pounds of marijuana every year. We get all our workers from the village and we pay them well, so they are loyal to us. There are forty heavily armed guards who live here and protect our assets." Musa was giddy. I love giving this tour, but I rarely get the opportunity.

"I must say that Stalin and you are perfectionists," said Leo.

Musa chuckled. "Last but not the least, are the eyes and ears of our organization." Musa's eyes twinkled. Musa tugged an iron ring on the wall that caused a panel in the ground to slide open. He turned around and winked. He walked down a flight of stairs and knocked on a door. It was opened by a young man who welcomed them in. There were two men in the room who monitored everything that happened inside Netherworld. There were sixteen monitors in the room, and the men could see every part of the underground structure. Every entry and exit had motion sensors that alerted the two men if there was any motion. If the men saw someone they didn't expect or recognize or noticed something out of the ordinary, they would sound the alarm. "There are two shifts," said Musa. "These guys are the second twelve-hour shift. That's all I have. Let's eat." Musa walked up the stairs.

"Musa, we have a plan to get Stalin out of Devil's Rock," said Leo once they were seated at the dining table.

"That place is like a fortress. I tried breaking in and failed." Musa came close to Leo. "What are you thinking?"

"We won't break in. We will have the prison warden bring him out," said Leo.

Musa had an expression of shock as he looked from Leo to Arnold. "Why on earth would the warden bring him out?"

"If Stalin gets very sick on Devil's Rock and the doctors in the infirmary cannot help him, they will take him to a government hospital on land," said Leo.

"How will Stalin get that sick?" Musa looked perplexed.

"My friend is working on a concoction of chemicals that will produce violent reactions in people when ingested in small amounts. They will begin to have muscle spasms for a few seconds and their vitals will go haywire. In measured small amounts, the body will react for a few seconds, and then everything will go back to normal." Leo had Musa's undivided attention.

"Your friend sounds like a dangerous man," said Musa. "I am going to ask the obvious question. How is Stalin going to get the chemical?"

"We are going to have a few of your guys deliver it to the prison," said

Leo nonchalantly.

"Stop screwing around," said Musa. He banged his fist on the table.

"My glass is empty, Musa. Get ready to fill it up once you hear this." Leo moved his whiskey glass toward Musa.

"There is a restaurant in the prison run by the warden. The waiters who work there are in Stalin's gang, and your people will get the chemical to a waiter who will get it to Stalin."

Musa stared from Leo to Arnold. "You guys are geniuses. Let me refill your glasses." Musa chuckled. "I have a bottle of twenty-one-year aged Glen Fiddich single malt scotch just for occasions like this."

A few days later, Leo went to Mumbai with Musa and two of Musa's men. The two men had bought dinner tickets to wine and dine at Devil's Rock and would take Walt's chemical to Stalin's man. Arnold stayed back at Netherworld and prepared for Stalin's arrival. Leo and Musa reached Mumbai and booked hotel rooms near the marina. Leo handed Musa a letter to give to Stalin with instructions about how the plan would be executed. "The escape is planned for Monday evening. I will bring you the chemical when it is ready."

Musa sipped on his scotch and stared out of his window.

Leo took leave and went to meet Isa.

The day Musa's men would enter Devil's Rock arrived. "Only two days till I see my brother," Musa told his men. "Make sure you deliver the chemicals and the letter. Stalin needs both for the plan to work. You will be handsomely rewarded." Musa's men headed to the meeting point where the boat would pick them up.

Musa's men entered Devil's Rock restaurant and seated themselves at one of the tables. One of the men wore a bracelet made of beads that held the chemicals Stalin needed to ingest. The bracelet had not been flagged as a security threat.

The waiter came over to the table where Musa's men sat. "What can I get you to drink?" He asked.

"Listen to me carefully. I am in Stalin's gang. I have some items I need you to get to him. Can you do that?"

The waiter glanced in all directions to make sure the guards weren't looking. "I am in Stalin's gang, and I will give him anything you want me to," said the waiter.

"I will leave my bracelet and a letter under my napkin on my dirty plate. Make sure Stalin gets the bracelet and the letter. You will be well rewarded." The man ordered a drink and an appetizer.

"Thank you, sir." I will make sure he gets them. The waiter went back to the kitchen.

After Musa's men had finished their appetizers, the waiter came to their table to take away the dirty plates. Musa's man signaled to his dirty plate with his eyes, and the waiter saw that he wasn't wearing his bracelet. The waiter took the plates into the kitchen. He lifted the napkin and found the bracelet and the letter.

"Nicely done," said Musa when his men told him that they had delivered the goods. "You guys go have some fun tonight." He gave each of the men a wad of cash.

***

Stalin sat at the cafeteria the next morning eating breakfast. The waiter who had the letter and bracelet went up to Stalin. "May I speak with you in private, sir?" the waiter asked Stalin.

"I'm having breakfast," said Stalin, sounding irritated.

"Sir, this is very important, and you really want to hear this. Trust me," said the man.

"This better be good." Stalin got up from his table and followed the man.

"You have some gifts from the outside, Stalin." The waiter looked around to make sure no one was watching and handed Stalin the bracelet and the letter.

Stalin took the items from the waiter. "You and your family will be rewarded for this." Stalin headed back to his cell and read the letter. A maniacal smile came across his face. Leo had delivered on his promise. It was only a matter of time before Stalin got out of this hell hole and wreaked havoc on the world.

The day of Stalin's escape arrived. The thought of getting out of Devil's Rock gave him an adrenaline rush. At the exact time listed on the letter, Stalin took out one of the beads from his bracelet and chewed on it. The effects of the chemical were instantaneous. He felt excruciating pain and convulsed. A couple of guards ran to Stalin and carried him to the infirmary.

The doctors checked Stalin's vitals and performed various tests.

Stalin followed the instruction on the letter and popped another bead into his mouth. He convulsed on the infirmary bed. Doctors scrambled to figure out what was happening. The sudden onset and conclusion of Stalin's symptoms flabbergasted the doctors. Stalin was placed under observation, and an attendant was assigned to monitor him.

Stalin ate two more beads. The doctors at the infirmary called the warden and informed him that Stalin needed to be transported to a hospital on land.

The warden made some calls and initiated the protocol to get Stalin transferred. Within twenty minutes, the warden, along with Stalin and two security guards, boarded the boat. Stalin was sedated and secured to a stretcher on the boat. One of the guards revved the engine, and the boat moved over choppy waters.

Musa and Leo waited on another boat close to the dock. There was a driver and another man on the boat. Leo looked through a pair of binoculars. "A boat with someone on a stretcher aboard just left the prison. It's got to be Stalin. This is it, Musa." He handed the binoculars to Musa.

Musa looked through the binoculars and laughed. "This is it. We are so close. Once your people take the security guards on the prison boat out, we'll get Stalin." The driver started the boat and slowly headed toward Stalin's boat.

The boat carrying Leo and Musa got close to Stalin's boat. There was a whizzing noise, and Musa collapsed. The older man on the boat walked to Musa's limp body. It was the director of Investigation Bureau. He put the tranquilizer gun back in his holster.

The prison boat came to a halt. Zubaria, who was driving the boat, anchored it next to the prison boat. The warden jumped onto Leo's boat.

"Thank you for your help on this, warden," said the director of Investigation Bureau, extending his hand. "I really appreciate what you have done for us. We wouldn't have been able to get Stalin and Musa without your help."

"I'm glad to help," said the warden, shaking the director's hand. "My prison was peaceful before Stalin became an inmate. Stalin started gang wars and is responsible for many deaths. I couldn't bear to have him in my prison. He is like a disease." The warden looked at Leo. "Nice work, Leo." He shook hands with Leo and then with Zubaria.

"I will make sure that we take care of this, warden. This will never come back to you," said the director. "You should wait for a few hours and head back to the prison. We will take care of the rest." The warden and his guards moved Stalin's stretcher onto the director's boat and disappeared into the night.

Zubaria drove the boat into the open ocean. Stalin and Musa woke up and found they were tied to metal chairs that rested on the stern railing of the boat. Stalin and Musa were both dazed from sedatives.

Stalin looked confused when he saw the skyline of Mumbai in a distance. "Where are we? Who the fuck are you?" yelled Stalin. He looked from the director to Zubaria.

The director paced the boat. "We are the last faces you will see in your godforsaken lives. I am the director of Investigation Bureau, an investigative organization funded by the prime minister. We are designed to take out criminals like you. This is my best agent, Zubaria, and this whole operation was her brainchild." The director pointed at Zubaria.

Stalin and Musa seethed.

"Where is Leo?" yelled Musa, his voice breaking as he looked around the boat.

"Leo was working for us the whole time," said Zubaria. "We recruited him after he pulled off an unbelievable bank robbery. We put him undercover on Devil's Rock, where he could infiltrate your organization. He went above and beyond our wildest expectations. Arnold is one of our agents, and I put him on Devil's Rock to take care of Leo in case anything went wrong." The ocean breeze blew Zubaria's hair, even though she wore a hat.

"I will destroy you and everyone in your family," screamed Musa. His eyes blazed.

"Listen to me carefully," said Zubaria. "Your organization no longer exists. Arnold, who was at your underground operation center, gave us the exact coordinates. Your operation was genius." Zubaria clapped her hands. "Without Leo and Arnold, we would never have been able to find your location and destroy everything you created. My team has taken most of your men captive and killed anyone who couldn't be captured alive. We have destroyed all your equipment, and there is nothing left of Netherworld but an empty shell." Zubaria's eyes blazed.

"The kid, Leo, was he not man enough to be here to finish the operation?" asked Stalin with an eerie calm. "Did he not have the courage to look me in the eye after betraying my trust?"

"Give him a break, Stalin. He is not used to death like you guys are," said the director, putting on gloves.

Stalin stopped struggling. "He is a smart kid and has a bright future," he said.

"I know, and I will make sure he reaches his true potential," said the director.

"You bastard. You will be answerable to us in the next life," screamed Musa.

"Musa, the death toll between the two of you runs in the thousands," replied the director. "You have murdered and destroyed the lives of men, women, and children. Your drugs have killed many or destroyed their lives. Before I answer to you in the next life, you will need to answer to all the people you killed." The director signaled to Zubaria, and she donned gloves.

"Why break me out, director? Why not just get me killed in the prison?" asked Stalin.

"Killing you in prison would create a huge gang war, and we didn't want to risk that. Your gang of imbeciles would attack and kill a bunch of inmates. The story we are going to tell everyone is that you died on the way to the hospital. Everyone saw you get very sick and won't have any trouble believing it. I already have a corpse that is going to be cremated and a story that everyone will know about the untimely death of Stalin because of an aneurysm." The director's eyes were cold.

Knowing that his fate was sealed, Stalin turned to Musa. "It was an honor to be by your side all these years. You are my brother." Stalin turned to the director and stared him in the eyes.

Stalin and Musa laughed maniacally.

The director and Zubaria undid the latches and folded the railing. Zubaria and the director simultaneously tipped over the metal chairs that held Stalin and Musa. Stalin and Musa continued to laugh maniacally while they fell over the side. There was a splash, and the laughter stopped. The director walked up to the edge of the boat and watched the heavy metal chairs disappear into the ocean.

The director came to the back of the boat. Leo sat on the floor looking grim. "I had never seen or heard anyone die before," said Leo. He shivered, partly because of the cold but mostly because of what he had witnessed.

"You did the right thing, Leo," said the director. "You've got to let it go. Those guys were scum, and they deserved to die."

"I can still hear their maniacal laughter," said Leo, cowering.

"Those men were singlehandedly responsible for the deaths of thousands of people. Their drugs have flooded the country and caused an epidemic that you helped cure. Stalin has killed many men in the prison just to satisfy his blood lust. You did your country a huge favor. Go home and spend time with your friends and loved ones and get some rest. Remember that in a month, you have your orientation as a special agent at Investigation Bureau. We have seized a huge amount of cash and gold from the vault in Stalin's organization, and you have earned a share for risking your life. It's not remotely close to what you took from the bank, but it should help you and your friends. Remember, this is a one-time deal, and the only reason you are getting paid is because you are a civilian and not yet an employee of Investigation Bureau. Once you become a special agent, you get paid your salary and benefits and nothing else besides the thrill of the chase and the pleasure of getting bad guys." The director sat down on the boat floor next to Leo.

Zubaria drove the boat to the pier.

The director dropped Leo at Isa's apartment. Leo got out of the car and bid Zubaria and the director goodbye.

Leo reached Isa's place and rang the doorbell. Isa opened the door and folded into his arms.

Leo felt warm. "This is exactly what I needed after the crazy night that I had," he told her.

Isa stayed in Leo's arms for a while. Leo took a long, hot shower and came out a different person. He got dressed, and they met the Sebastian and Walt downstairs. They went to the neighborhood bar and ordered drinks.

The director had helped Sebastian get a job as an engineer in a new car company located just outside of Mumbai. Sebastian was going to be the engineer he and his family had dreamed he would become.

Isa was making a difference in the lives of many women, and she had become a celebrity. She had been featured on the cover of a popular magazine as one of the youngest people to become an agent of change. She was interviewed on television where she was celebrated as a superhero for making a difference and saving lives.

Walt was Isa's second in command and was head of operations at Aashray. He had reconciled his differences with his father. His father visited him in Mumbai occasionally, and he visited his father back home as well.

In one month, Leo would become Special Agent Leonardo Varma at Investigation Bureau and solve crimes and get justice. The deal he had made with Zubaria and the director had saved his friends from going to prison. The deal also helped him achieve his goal of punishing criminals. He would have unlimited resources and get paid to catch criminals.

The four of them sat at the bar and drank the night away. Destiny had changed the course of Leo's life, but he was exactly where he was meant to be. Leo was with the woman he loved and hoped to marry one day. He was also with two of his dearest friends. He raised his glass and made a toast. "To family."

Made in the USA
Middletown, DE
16 December 2021

56263641R00128